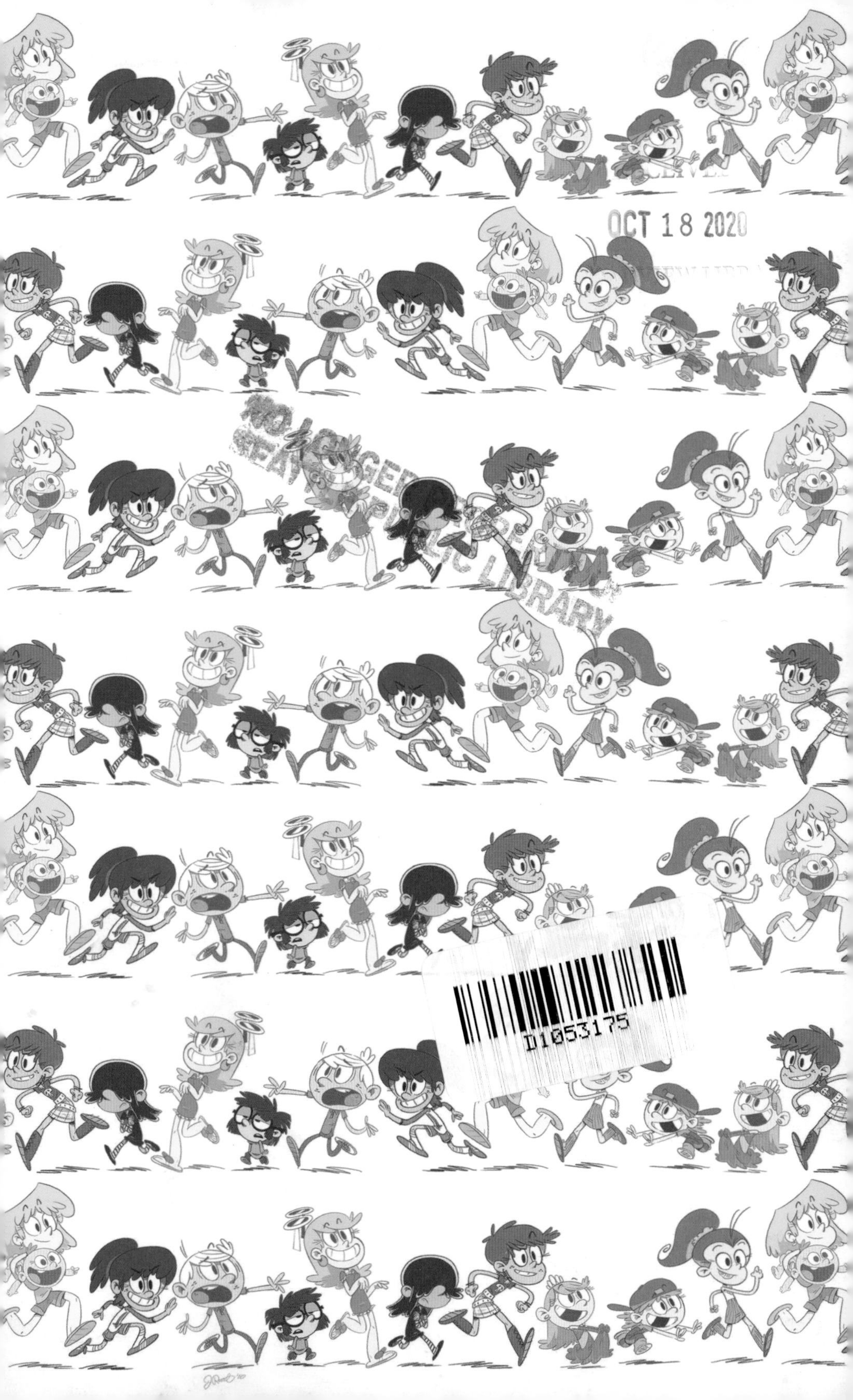

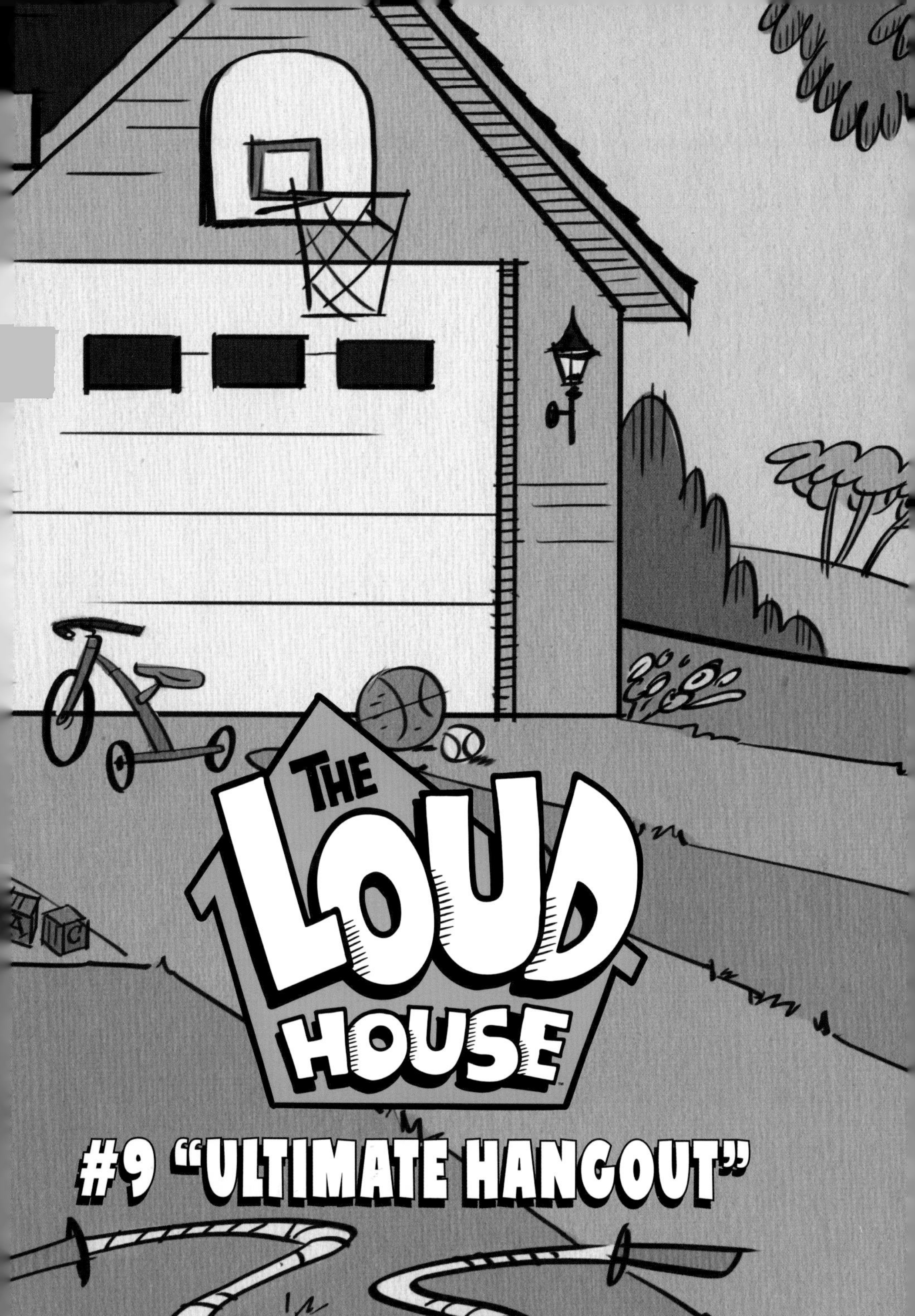

THE LOUD HOUSE

#9 "ULTIMATE HANGOUT"

PAPERCUTZ
New York

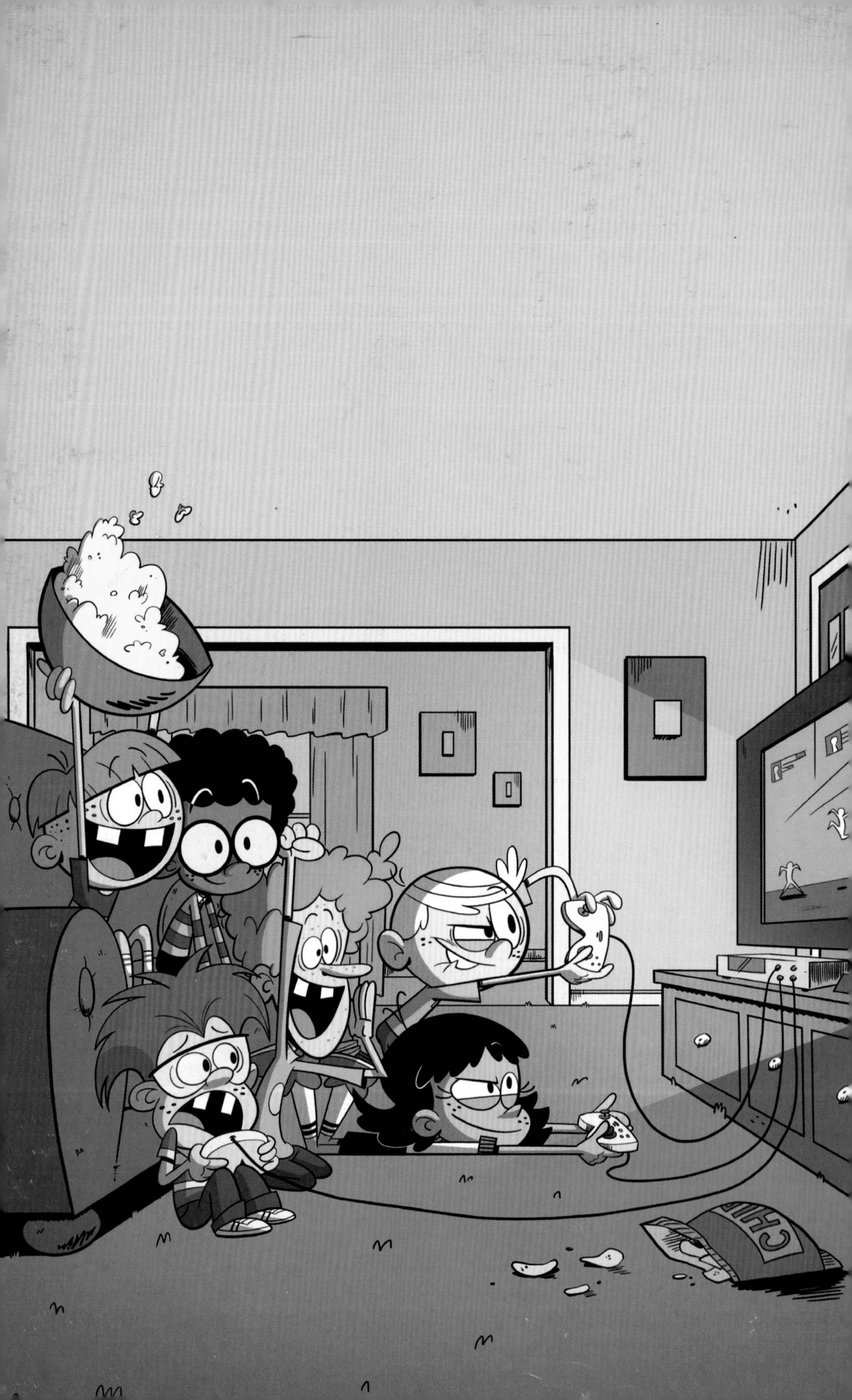

THE LOUD HOUSE

#9 "ULTIMATE HANGOUT"

nickelodeon™ THE LOUD HOUSE

#9 "ULTIMATE HANGOUT"

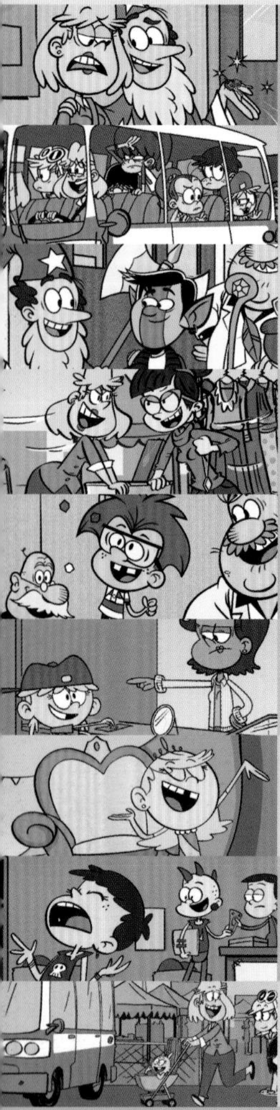

"THE EMPTY LOUD HOUSE"
Jeff Sayers — Writer
Zazo Aguiar — Artist, Colorist
Wilson Ramos Jr. — Letterer

"THE SAUCY LINE"
Jeff Sayers — Writer
Zazo Aguiar — Artist
Zazo Aguiar, Vic Miyuki — Colorists
Wilson Ramos Jr. — Letterer

"SPACE RACE"
Andrew Brooks — Writer
Erin Hyde — Artist, Colorist
Wilson Ramos Jr. — Letterer

"NO STRINGS"
Caitlin Fein — Writer
Kelsey Wooley — Artist, Colorist
Wilson Ramos Jr. — Letterer

"DIVIDE AND CONQUER"
Sammie Crowley — Writer
Zazo Aguiar — Artist, Colorist
Wilson Ramos Jr. — Letterer

"SLAM JUNK"
Sammie Crowley — Writer
Gizelle Orbino — Artist, Colorist
Wilson Ramos Jr. — Letterer

"HAGGLE TALE"
Andrew Brooks — Writer
Lee-Roy Lahey — Artist, Colorist
Wilson Ramos Jr. — Letterer

"IT'S MY PARTY"
Caitlin Fein — Writer
Zazo Aguiar — Artist, Colorist
Wilson Ramos Jr. — Letterer

"PARTY HOPPERS"
Andrew Brooks — Writer
Zazo Aguiar — Artist, Colorist
Wilson Ramos Jr. — Letterer

"EYE ON THE BALL"
Caitlin Fein — Writer
Daniela Rodriguez — Artist, Colorist
Wilson Ramos Jr. — Letterer

"THE FLEA MARKET"
Jeff Sayers— Writer
Ronda Pattison — Artist, Colorist
Wilson Ramos Jr. — Letterer

"THE PERFECT GIFT"
Katie Mattila — Writer
Max Alley — Artist
JayJay Jackson— Colorist
Wilson Ramos Jr. — Letterer

"RACE TO THE THRONE"
Katie Mattila— Writer
Daniela Rodriguez — Artist, Colorist
Wilson Ramos Jr. — Letterer

"FLEA RIDDLE"
Jeff Sayers — Writer
Max Alley — Artist
Ronda Pattison — Colorist
Wilson Ramos Jr. — Letterer

"RECORD TIME"
Caitlin Fein — Writer
Daniela Rodriguez — Artist, Colorist
Wilson Ramos Jr. — Letterer

"PARTY MIXER"
Katie Mattila — Writer
Zazo Aguiar — Artist, Colorist
Wilson Ramos Jr. — Letterer

"THE LONG ROAD HOME"
Katie Mattila — Writer
Gizelle Orbino — Artist, Colorist
Wilson Ramos Jr. — Letterer

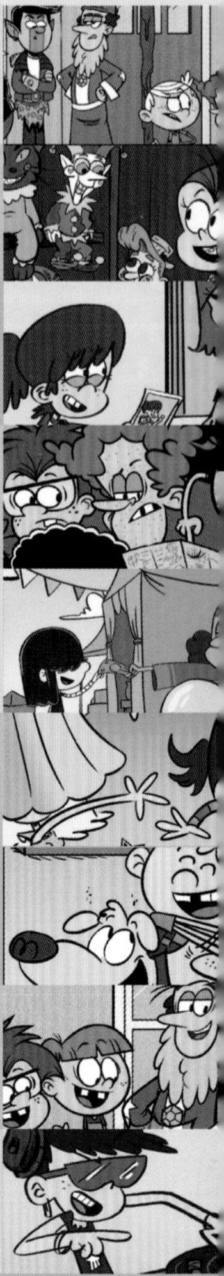

IDA HEM — Cover Artist
HALLIE LAL — Cover Colorist
JORDAN ROSATO — Endpapers
JAMES SALERNO — Sr. Art Director/Nickelodeon
JAYJAY JACKSON — Design
SAMMIE CROWLEY, SEAN GANTKA, ANGELA ENTZMINGER, DANA CLUVERIUS, MOLLIE FREILICH — Special Thanks
JEFF WHITMAN — Editor
JOAN HILTY — Editor/Nickelodeon
JIM SALICRUP
Editor-in-Chief

ISBN: 978-1-5458-0405-6 paperback edition
ISBN: 978-1-5458-0406-3 hardcover edition

www.papercutz.com

Papercutz books may be purchased for business or promotional use. For information on bulk purchases please contact Macmillan Corporate anc Premium Sales Department at (800) 221-7945 x5442.

Printed in China
April 2020

Distributed by Macmillan
First Printing

MEET THE LOUD FAMILY

and friends!

LINCOLN LOUD
THE MIDDLE CHILD (11)

At 11 years old, Lincoln is the middle child, with five older sisters and five younger sisters. He has learned that surviving the Loud household means staying a step ahead. He's the man with a plan, always coming up with a way to get what he wants or deal with a problem, even if things inevitably go wrong. Being the only boy comes with some perks. Lincoln gets his own room – even if it's just a converted linen closet. On the other hand, being the only boy also means he sometimes gets a little too much attention from his sisters. They mother him, tease him, and use him as the occasional lab rat or fashion show participant. Lincoln's sisters may drive him crazy, but he loves them and is always willing to help out if they need him.

LORI LOUD
THE OLDEST (17)

As the first-born child of the Loud Clan, Lori sees herself as the boss of all her siblings. She feels she's paved the way for them and deserves extra respect. Her signature traits are rolling her eyes, texting her boyfriend, Bobby, and literally saying "literally" all the time. Because she's the oldest and most experienced sibling, Lori can be a great ally, so it pays to stay on her good side, especially since she can drive.

LENI LOUD
THE FASHIONISTA (16)

Leni spends most of her time designing outfits and accessorizing. She always falls for Luan's pranks, and sometimes walks into walls when she's talking (she's not great at doing two things at once). Leni might be flighty, but she's the sweetest of the Loud siblings and truly has a heart of gold (even though she's pretty sure it's a heart of blood).

LUNA LOUD
THE ROCK STAR (15)

Luna is loud, boisterous and freewheeling, and her energy is always cranked to 11. She thinks about music so much that she even talks in song lyrics. On the off-chance she doesn't have her guitar with her, everything can and will be turned into a musical instrument. You can always count on Luna to help out, and she'll do most anything you ask, as long as you're okay with her supplying a rocking guitar accompaniment.

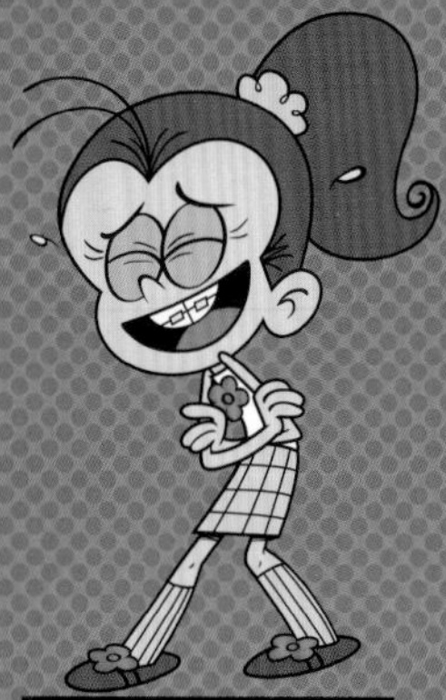

LUAN LOUD
THE JOKESTER (14)

Luan's a standup comedienne who provides a nonstop barrage of silly puns. She's big on prop comedy too – squirting flowers and whoopee cushions – so you have to be on your toes whenever she's around. She loves to pull pranks and is a really good ventriloquist – she is often found doing bits with her dummy, Mr. Coconuts. Luan never lets anything get her down; to her, laughter IS the best medicine.

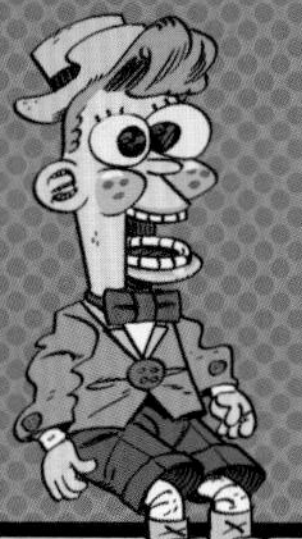

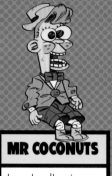

MR COCONUTS

Luan Loud's wise-cracking dummy.

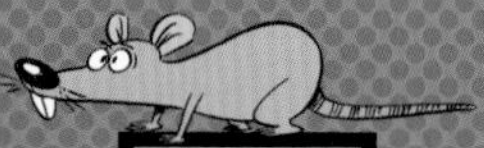

BITEY

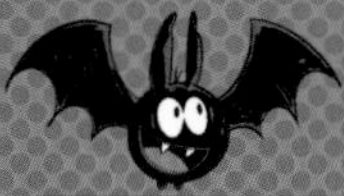

FANGS

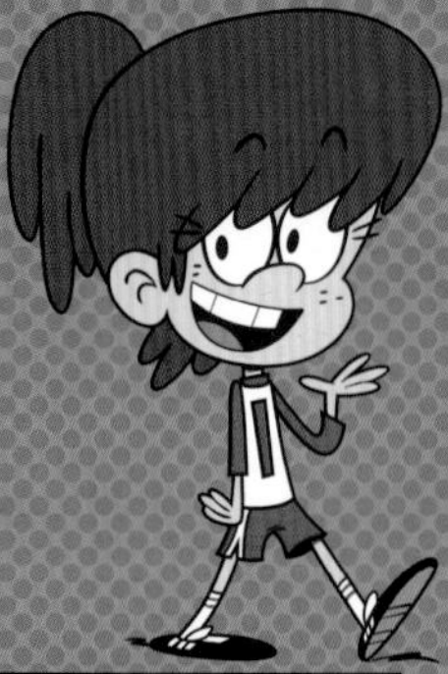

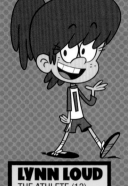

LYNN LOUD
THE ATHLETE (13)

Lynn is athletic and full of energy and is always looking for a teammate. With her, it's all sports all the time. She'll turn anything into a sport. Putting away eggs? Jump shot! Score! Cleaning up the eggs? Slap shot! Score! Lynn is very competitive, but despite her competitive nature, she always tries to just have a good time.

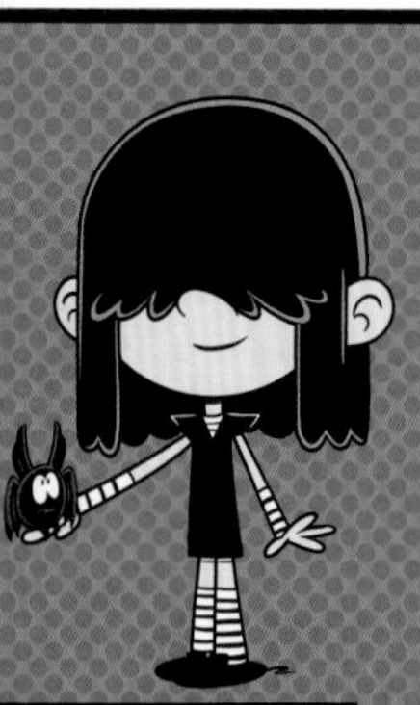

LUCY LOUD
THE EMO (8)

You can always count on Lucy to give the morbid point of view in any given situation. She is obsessed with all things spooky and dark – funerals, vampires, séances, and the like. She wears mostly black and writes moody poetry. She's usually quiet and keeps to herself. Lucy has a way of mysteriously appearing out of nowhere, and try as they might, her siblings never get used to this.

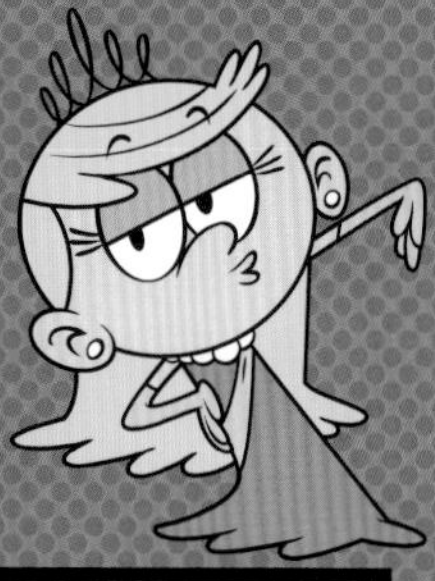

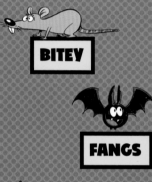

LOLA LOUD
THE BEAUTY QUEEN (6)

Lola could not be more different from her twin sister, Lana. She's a pageant powerhouse whose interests include glitter, photo shoots, and her own beautiful, beautiful face. But don't let her cute, gap-toothed smile fool you; underneath all the sugar and spice lurks a Machiavellian mastermind. Whatever Lola wants, Lola gets – or else. She's the eyes and ears of the household and never resists an opportunity to tattle on troublemakers. But if you stay on Lola's good side, you've got yourself a fierce ally – and a lifetime supply of free makeovers.

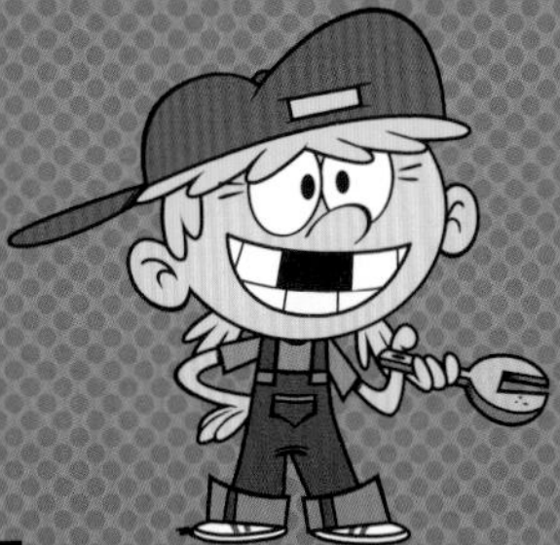

LANA LOUD
THE TOMBOY (6)

Lana is the rough-and-tumble sparkplug counterpart to her twin sister, Lola. She's all about reptiles, mud pies, and muffler repair. She's the resident Ms. Fix-it and is always ready to lend a hand – the dirtier the job, the better. Need your toilet unclogged? Snake fed? Back-zit popped? Lana's your gal. All she asks in return is a little A-B-C gum, or a handful of kibble (she often sneaks it from the dog bowl).

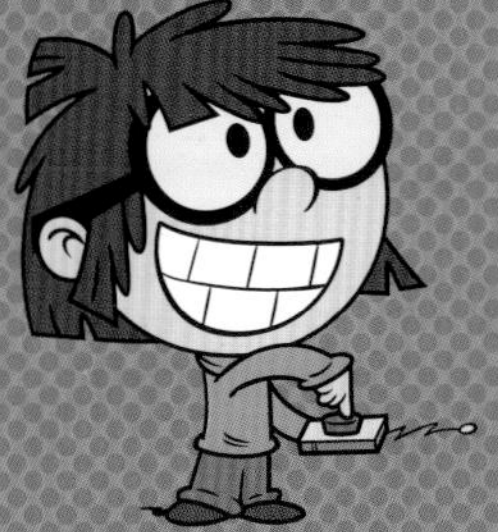

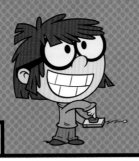

LISA LOUD
THE GENIUS (4)

Lisa is smarter than the rest of her siblings combined. She'll most likely be a rocket scientist, or a brain surgeon, or an evil genius who takes over the world. Lisa spends most of her time working in her lab (the family has gotten used to the explosions), and says her research leaves little time for frivolous human pursuits like "playing" or "getting haircuts." That said, she's always there to help with a homework question, or to explain why the sky is blue, or to point out the structural flaws in someone's pillow fort. Lisa says it's the least she can do for her favorite test subjects, er, siblings.

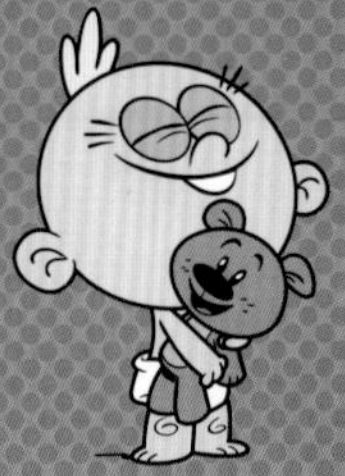

LILY LOUD
THE BABY (15 MONTHS)

Lily is a giggly, drooly, diaper-ditching free spirit, affectionately known as "the poop machine." You can't keep a nappy on this kid – she's like a teething Houdini. But even when Lily's running wild, dropping rancid diaper bombs, or drooling all over the remote, she always brings a smile to everyone's face (and a clothespin to their nose). Lily is everyone's favorite little buddy, and the whole family loves her unconditionally.

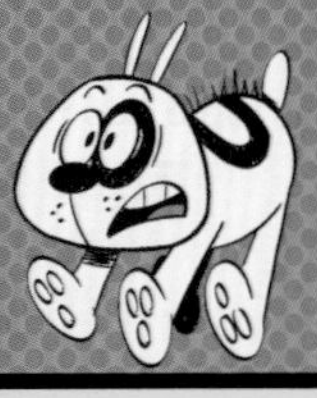

CHARLES

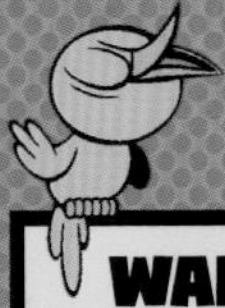

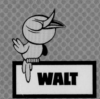

WALT

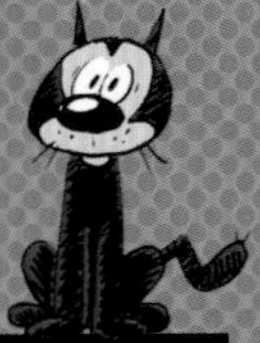

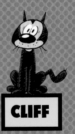

CLIFF

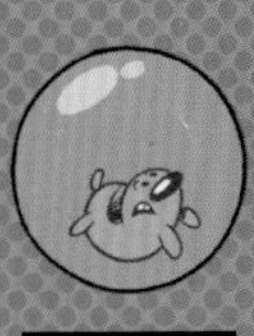

GEO

RITA LOUD

Mother to the eleven Loud kids, Mom (Rita Loud) wears many different hats. She's a chauffeur, homework-checker and barf-cleaner-upper all rolled into one. She's always there for her kids and ready to jump into action during a crisis, whether it's a fight between the twins or Leni's missing shoe. When she's not chasing the kids around or at her day job as a dental hygienist, Mom pursues her passion: writing. She also loves taking on house projects and is very handy with tools (guess that's where Lana gets it from). Between writing, working and being a mom, her days are always hectic but she wouldn't have it any other way.

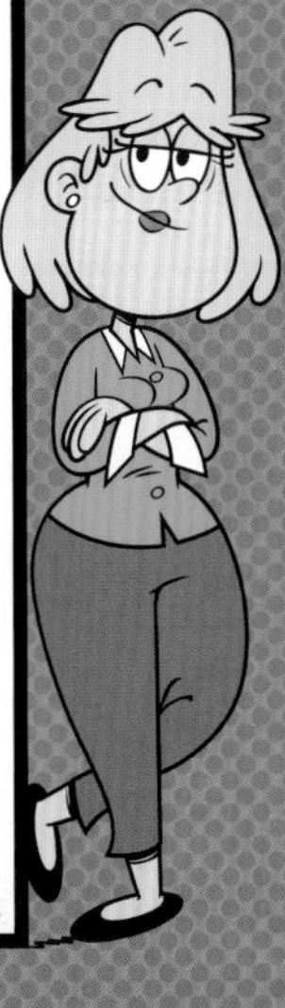

LYNN LOUD SR.

Dad (Lynn Loud Sr.) is a fun-loving, upbeat aspiring chef. A kid-at-heart, he's not above taking part in the kids' zany schemes. In addition to cooking, Dad loves his van, playing the cowbell and making puns. Before meeting Mom, Dad spent a semester in England and has been obsessed with British culture ever since – and sometimes "accidentally" slips into a British accent. When Dad's not wrangling the kids, he's pursuing his dream of opening his own restaurant where he hopes to make his "Lynn-sagnas" world-famous.

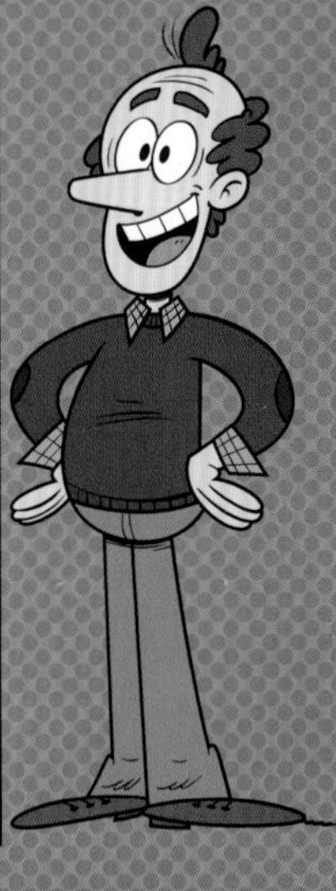

MR. BUD GROUSE

Mr. Grouse is the Louds's next-door-neighbor. The Louds often go to him for favors which he normally rejects – unless there's a chance for him to score one of Dad's famous Lynn-sagnas. Mr. Grouse loves gardening, relaxing in his recliner and keeping anything of the Louds's that flies into his yard (his catchphrase, after all, is "my yard, my property!").

POP POP

Albert, the Loud kids' grandfather, currently lives at Sunset Canyon Retirement Community after dedicating his life to working in the military. Pop Pop spends his days dominating at shuffleboard, eating pudding and going on adventures with his pals Bernie, Scoots, and Seymour and his girlfriend, Myrtle. Pop Pop is upbeat, fun-loving and cherishes spending time with his grandchildren.

FLIP

The owner of Flip's Food & Fuel, the local convenience store. Flip has questionable business practices – he's been known to sell expired milk and stick his feet in the nacho cheese! When he's not selling Flippees, Flip loves fishing and also sponsors Lynn's rec basketball team.

HAROLD McBRIDE
CLYDE'S DAD

Harold, one of Clyde's Dads, is a level-headed straight-shooter with a heart of gold. The more easygoing of Clyde's dads, Harold often has to convince Howard that it's okay for them to not constantly hover over Clyde. Harold also has an athletic side – he played baseball in college and he and Howard are always up for challenging themselves physically, going as far as to take part in the Royal Woods Samurai Warrior competition.

HOWARD McBRIDE
CLYDE'S OTHER DAD

Howard, Clyde's other Dad, is a constantly anxious helicopter parent. Howard is emotional, whether it be sad times (like when Clyde stubbed his toe) or happy (like when Clyde and Lincoln beat that really tough video game). Howard is endlessly supportive of Clyde and is always by his side (watching to make sure nothing goes wrong). When he's not watching Clyde's every move, he's taking care of the McBrides' cats, Cleopawtra and Nepurrtiti or playing the jazz saxophone.

KOTARO

Kotaro is Lynn Sr.'s best friend. He works at Lynn's Table. A lover of cowbell music, Kotaro is in a cowbell band along with Lynn Sr.—The Bell Boyz.

CLYDE McBRIDE
THE BEST FRIEND (11)

Clyde is Lincoln's partner in crime. He's always willing to go along with Lincoln's crazy schemes (even if he sees the flaws in them up-front). Lincoln and Clyde are two peas in a pod and share pretty much all of the same tastes in movies, comics, TV shows, toys—you name it. As an only child, Clyde envies Lincoln—how cool would it be to always have siblings around to talk to? But since Clyde spends so much time at the Loud household, he's almost an honorary sibling anyway.

RUSTY SPOKES

Rusty is a self-proclaimed ladies' man who's always the first to dish out girl advice—even though he's never been on an actual date. His dad owns a suit rental service, so occasionally Rusty can hook the gang up with some dapper duds—just as long as no one gets anything dirty.

ZACH GURDLE

Zach is a self-admitted nerd who's obsessed with aliens and conspiracy theories. He lives between a freeway and a circus, so the chaos of the Loud House doesn't faze him. He and Rusty occasionally butt heads, but deep down, it's all love.

LIAM

Liam is an enthusiastic, sweet-natured farm boy full of down-home wisdom. He loves hanging out with his Mee Maw, wrestling his prize pig Virginia, and sharing his farm-to-table produce with the rest of the gang.

STELLA

Stella, 11, is a quirky, carefree girl who's new to Royal Woods. She has tons of interests, like trying on wigs, playing laser tag, eating curly fries, and hanging with her friends. But what she loves the most is tech — she always wants to dismantle electronics and put them back together again.

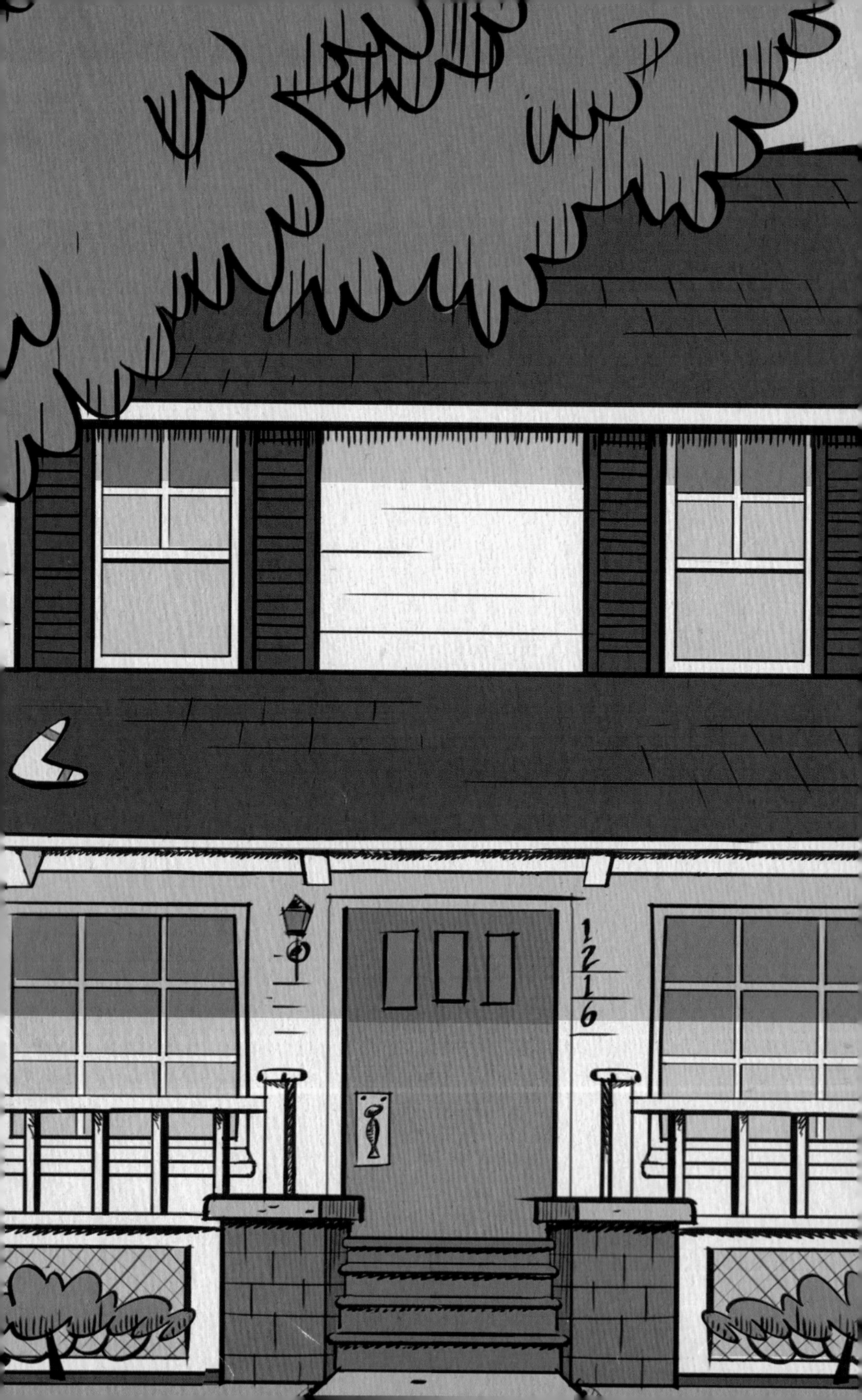
1216

"THE EMPTY LOUD HOUSE"

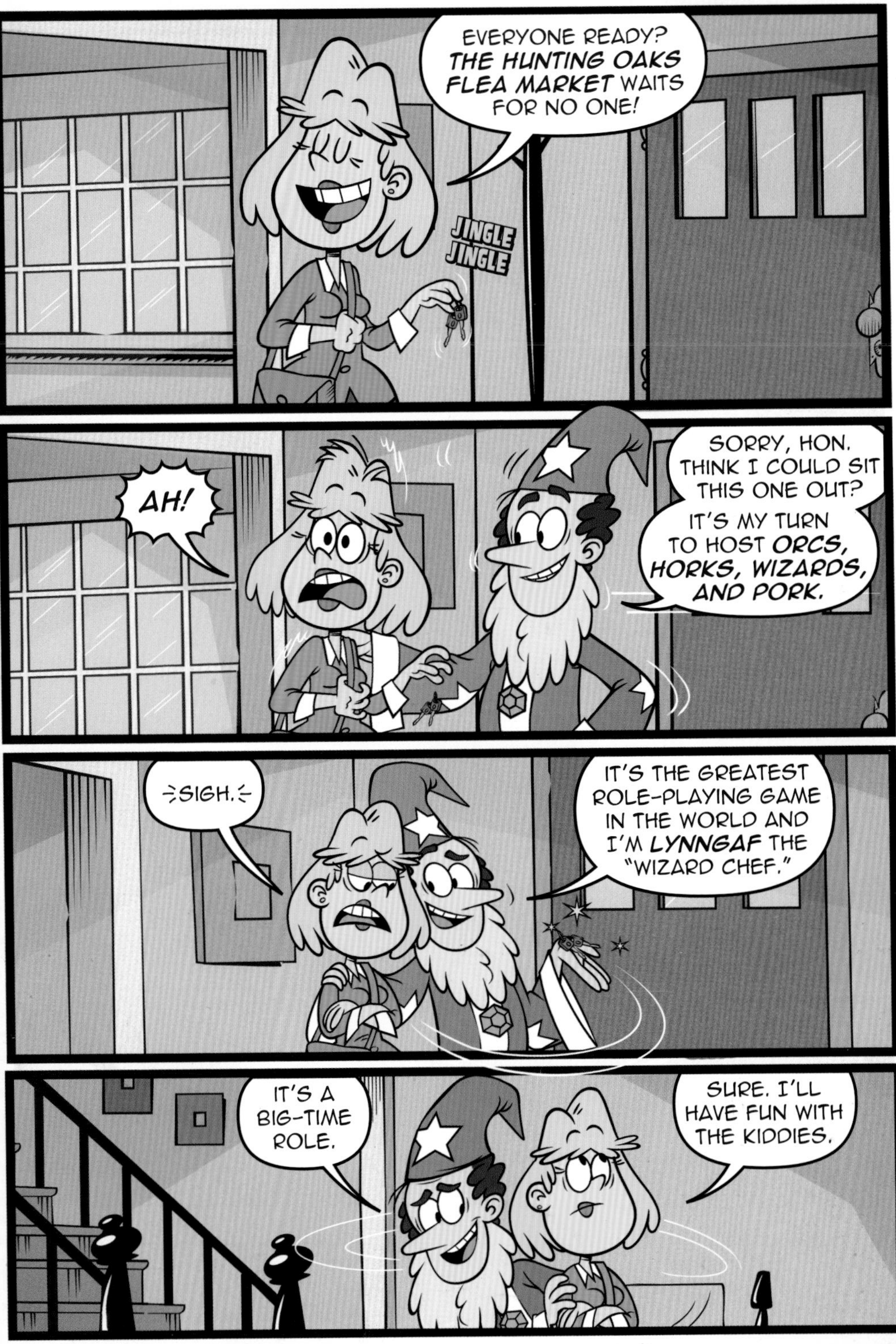
EVERYONE READY? THE HUNTING OAKS FLEA MARKET WAITS FOR NO ONE!
JINGLE JINGLE
AH!
SORRY, HON. THINK I COULD SIT THIS ONE OUT?
IT'S MY TURN TO HOST ORCS, HORKS, WIZARDS, AND PORK.
SIGH.
IT'S THE GREATEST ROLE-PLAYING GAME IN THE WORLD AND I'M LYNNGAF THE "WIZARD CHEF."
IT'S A BIG-TIME ROLE.
SURE. I'LL HAVE FUN WITH THE KIDDIES.

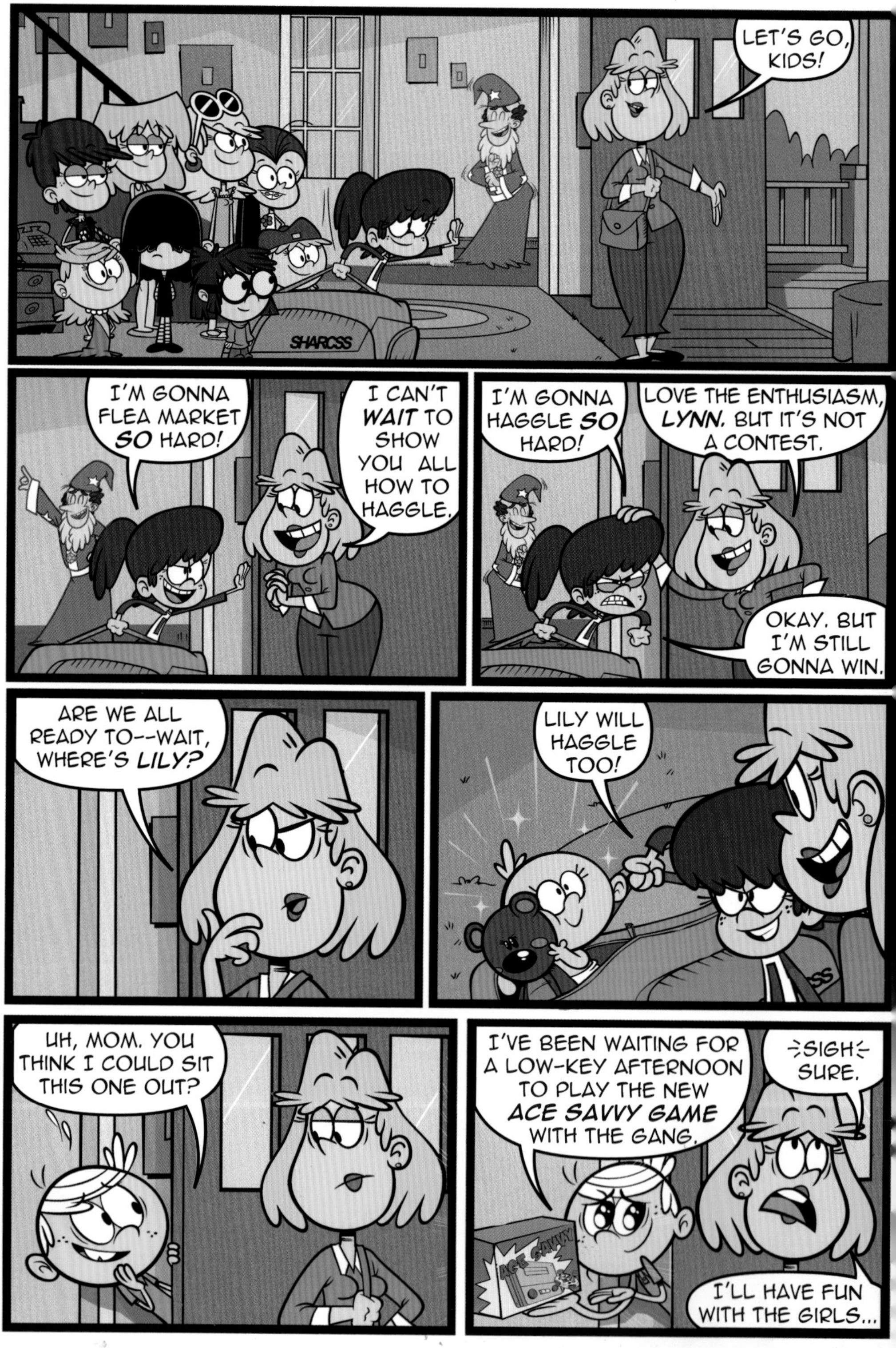

LET'S GO, KIDS!
I'M GONNA FLEA MARKET SO HARD!
I CAN'T WAIT TO SHOW YOU ALL HOW TO HAGGLE.
I'M GONNA HAGGLE SO HARD!
LOVE THE ENTHUSIASM, LYNN. BUT IT'S NOT A CONTEST.
OKAY. BUT I'M STILL GONNA WIN.
ARE WE ALL READY TO--WAIT, WHERE'S LILY?
LILY WILL HAGGLE TOO!
UH, MOM. YOU THINK I COULD SIT THIS ONE OUT?
I'VE BEEN WAITING FOR A LOW-KEY AFTERNOON TO PLAY THE NEW ACE SAVVY GAME WITH THE GANG.
SIGH SURE.
I'LL HAVE FUN WITH THE GIRLS...

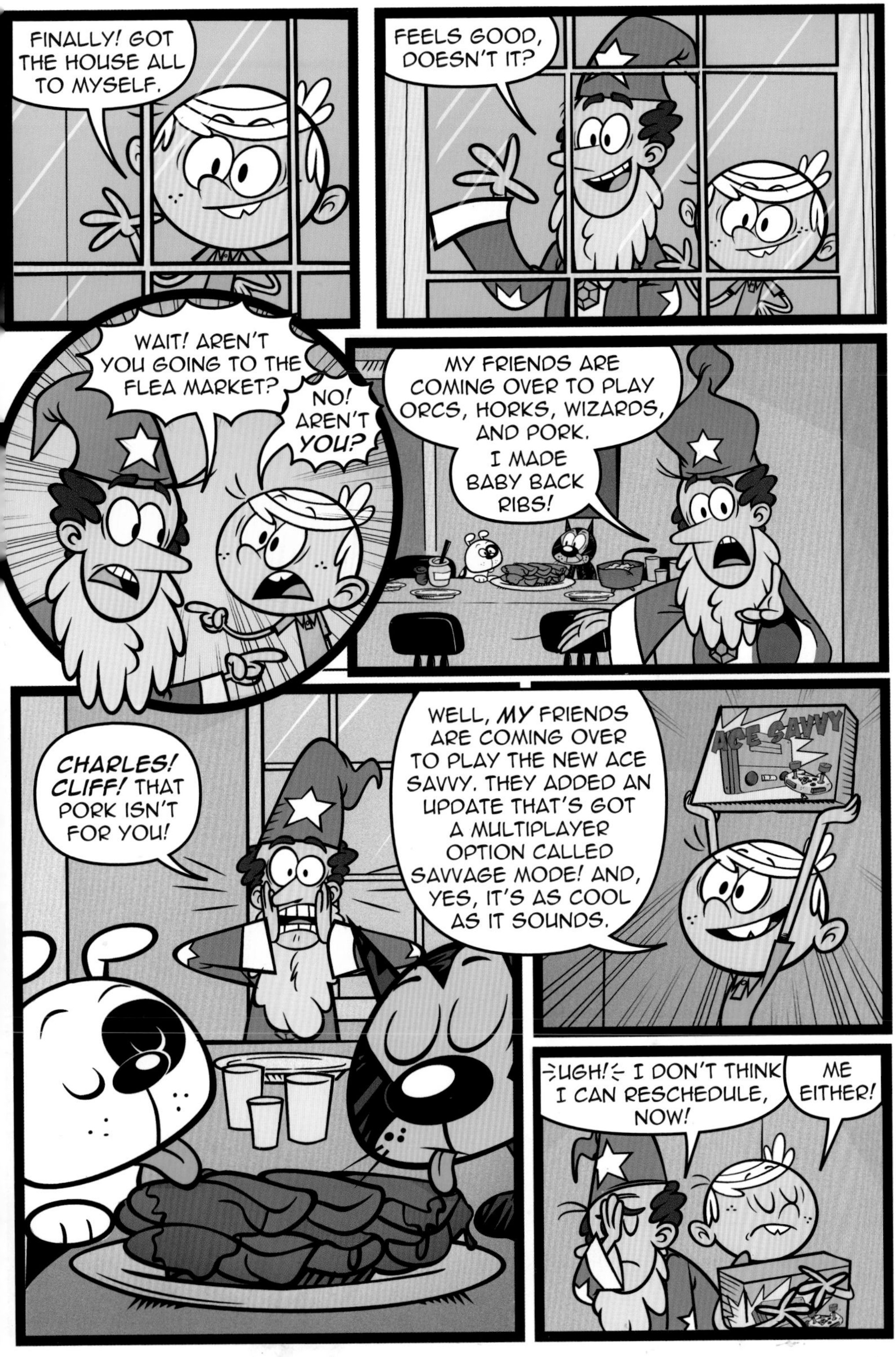
FINALLY! GOT THE HOUSE ALL TO MYSELF.
FEELS GOOD, DOESN'T IT?
WAIT! AREN'T YOU GOING TO THE FLEA MARKET?
NO! AREN'T *YOU?*
MY FRIENDS ARE COMING OVER TO PLAY ORCS, HORKS, WIZARDS, AND PORK.
I MADE BABY BACK RIBS!
WELL, *MY* FRIENDS ARE COMING OVER TO PLAY THE NEW ACE SAVVY. THEY ADDED AN UPDATE THAT'S GOT A MULTIPLAYER OPTION CALLED SAVVAGE MODE! AND, YES, IT'S AS COOL AS IT SOUNDS.
ACE SAVVY
CHARLES! CLIFF! THAT PORK ISN'T FOR YOU!
UGH! I DON'T THINK I CAN RESCHEDULE, NOW!
ME EITHER!

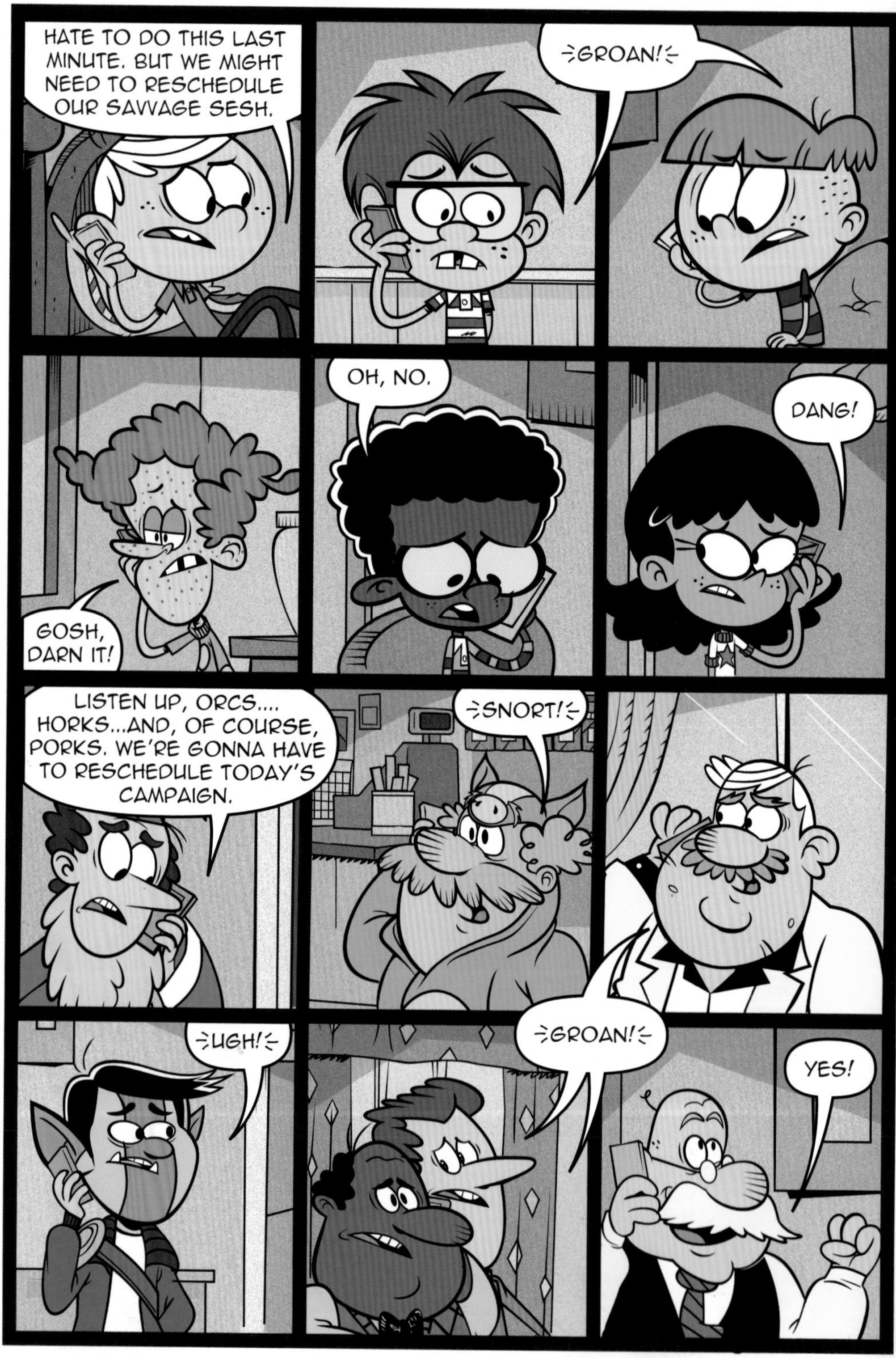
HATE TO DO THIS LAST MINUTE. BUT WE MIGHT NEED TO RESCHEDULE OUR SAVVAGE SESH.
GROAN!
OH, NO.
GOSH, DARN IT!
DANG!
LISTEN UP, ORCS.... HORKS...AND, OF COURSE, PORKS. WE'RE GONNA HAVE TO RESCHEDULE TODAY'S CAMPAIGN.
SNORT!
UGH!
GROAN!
YES!

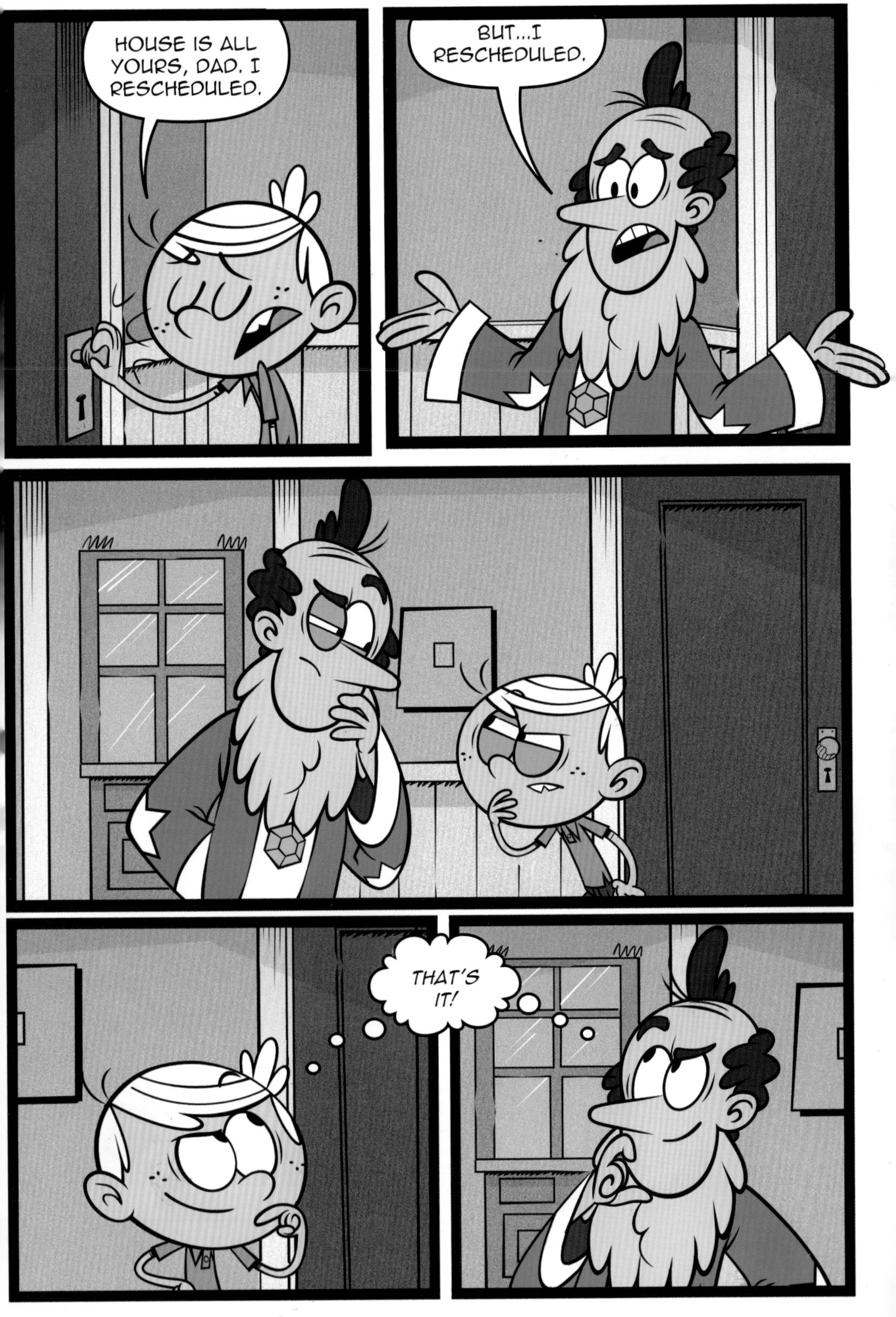
HOUSE IS ALL YOURS, DAD. I RESCHEDULED.
BUT...I RESCHEDULED.
THAT'S IT!

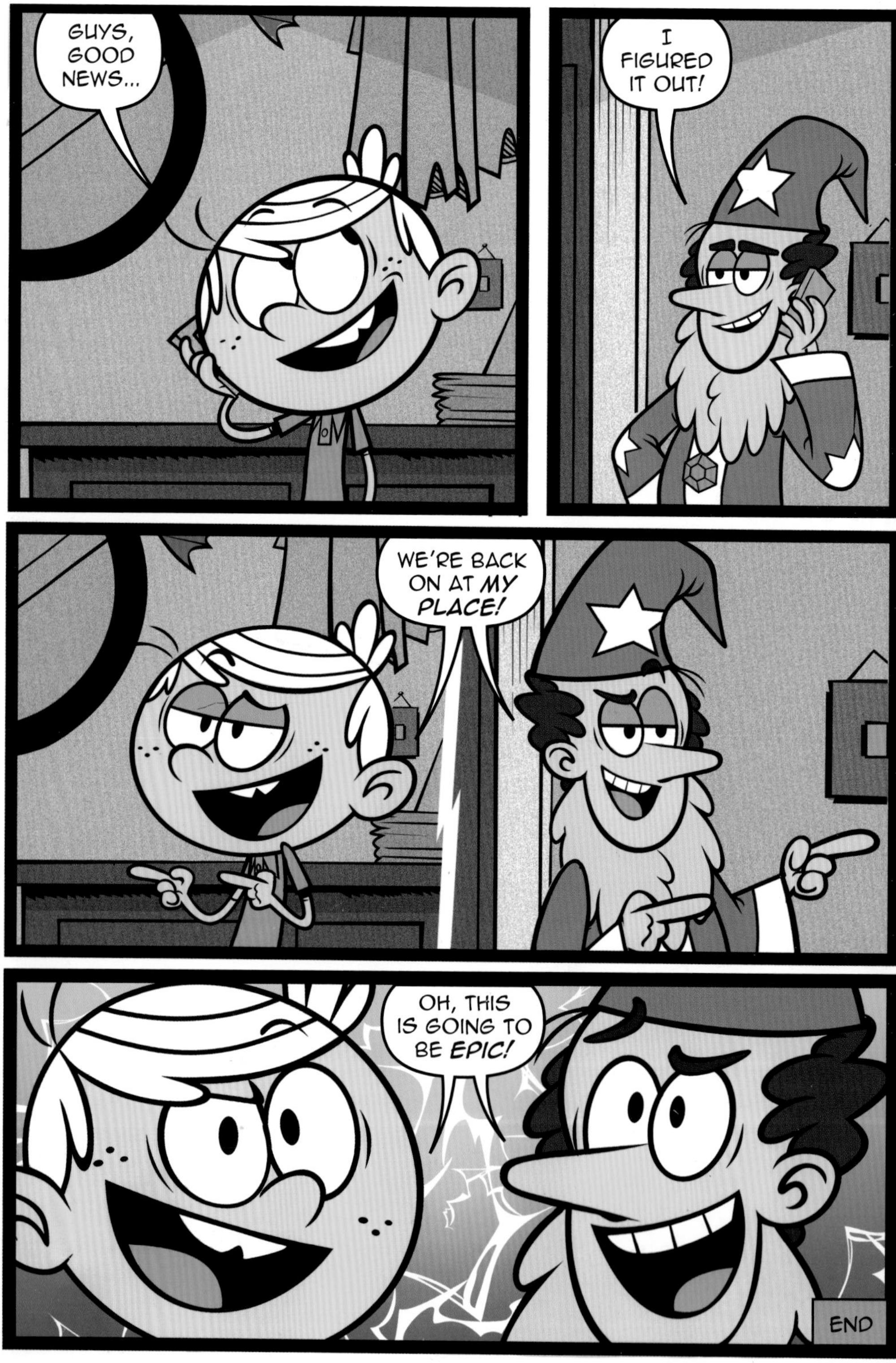
GUYS, GOOD NEWS...
I FIGURED IT OUT!
WE'RE BACK ON AT *MY PLACE!*
OH, THIS IS GOING TO BE *EPIC!*
END

"SPACE RACE"

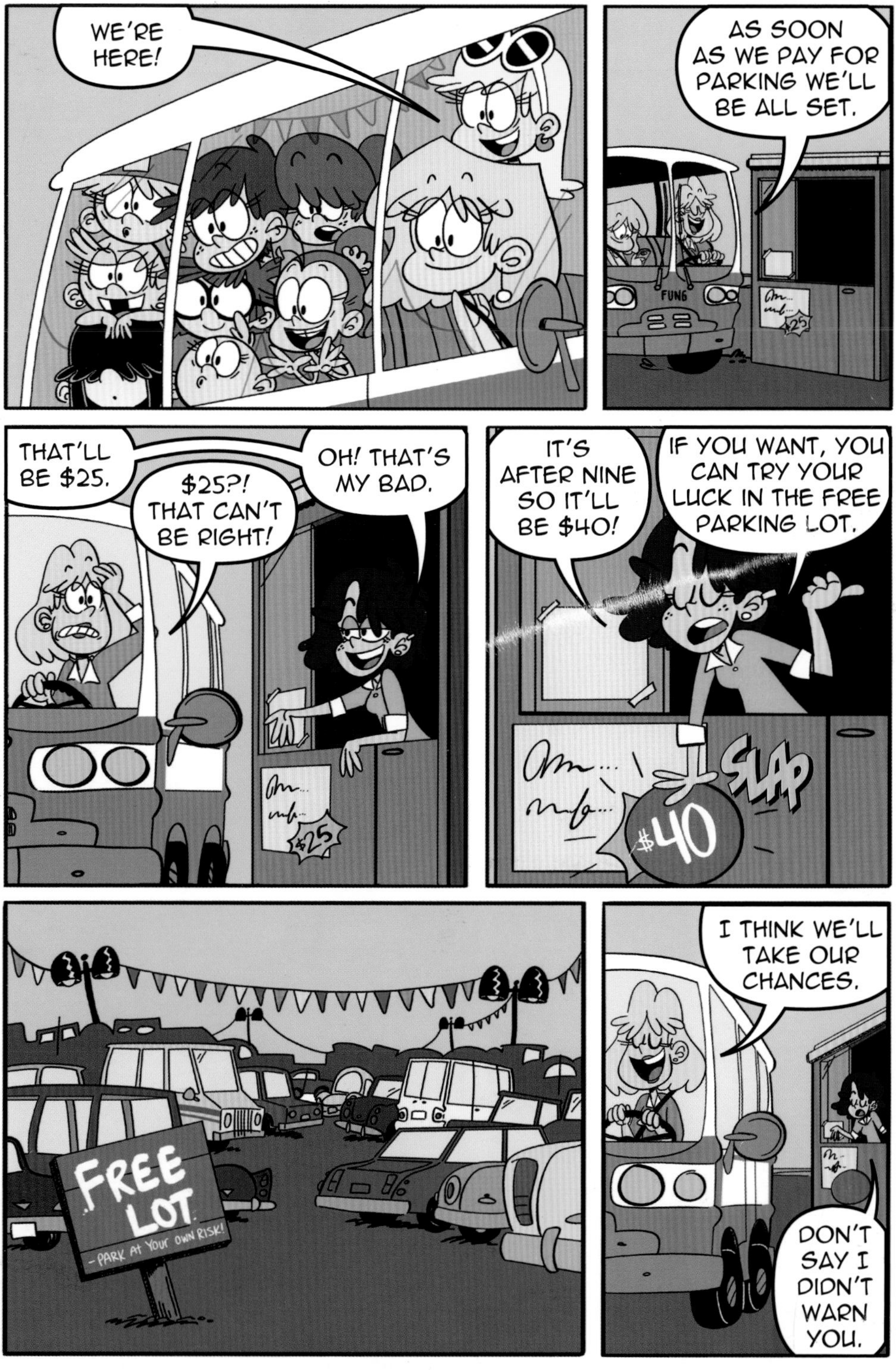

WE'RE HERE!
AS SOON AS WE PAY FOR PARKING WE'LL BE ALL SET.
FUNG
$25
THAT'LL BE $25.
$25?! THAT CAN'T BE RIGHT!
OH! THAT'S MY BAD.
$25
IT'S AFTER NINE SO IT'LL BE $40!
IF YOU WANT, YOU CAN TRY YOUR LUCK IN THE FREE PARKING LOT.
SLAP
$40
FREE LOT
- PARK AT YOUR OWN RISK!
I THINK WE'LL TAKE OUR CHANCES.
DON'T SAY I DIDN'T WARN YOU.

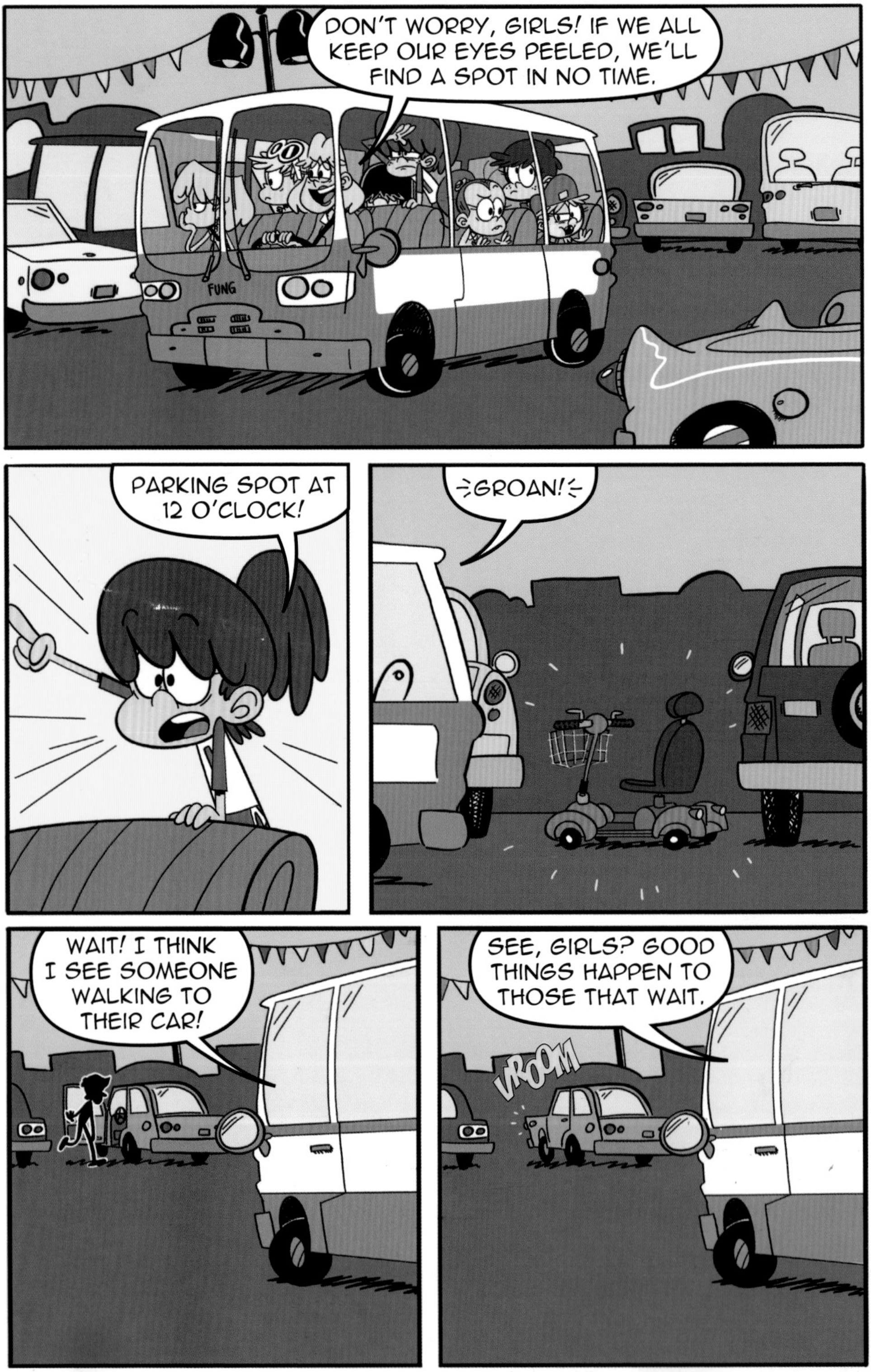
DON'T WORRY, GIRLS! IF WE ALL KEEP OUR EYES PEELED, WE'LL FIND A SPOT IN NO TIME.
FUNG
PARKING SPOT AT 12 O'CLOCK!
GROAN!
WAIT! I THINK I SEE SOMEONE WALKING TO THEIR CAR!
SEE, GIRLS? GOOD THINGS HAPPEN TO THOSE THAT WAIT.
VROOM

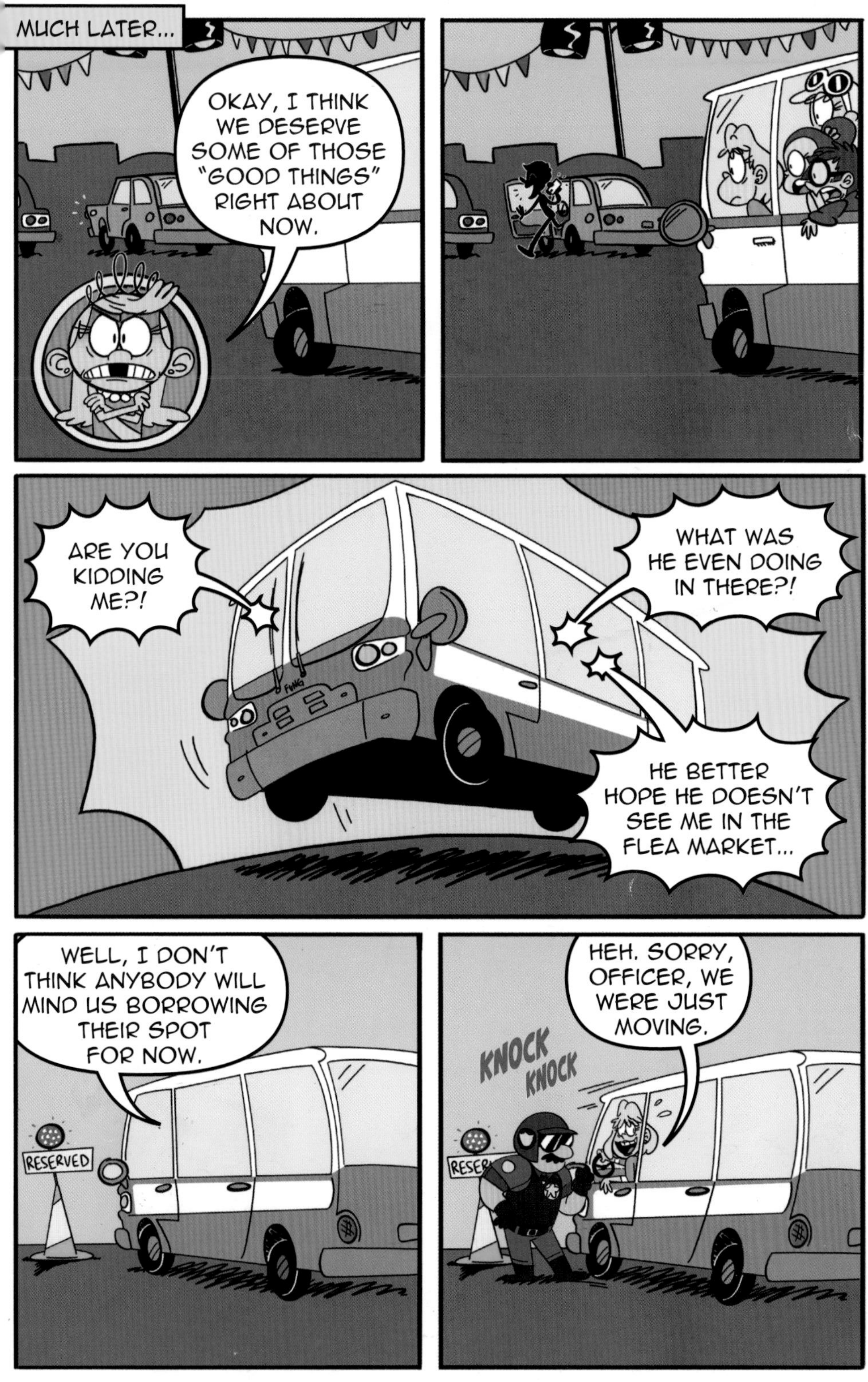
MUCH LATER...
OKAY, I THINK WE DESERVE SOME OF THOSE "GOOD THINGS" RIGHT ABOUT NOW.
ARE YOU KIDDING ME?!
WHAT WAS HE EVEN DOING IN THERE?!
HE BETTER HOPE HE DOESN'T SEE ME IN THE FLEA MARKET...
WELL, I DON'T THINK ANYBODY WILL MIND US BORROWING THEIR SPOT FOR NOW.
RESERVED
KNOCK KNOCK
HEH. SORRY, OFFICER, WE WERE JUST MOVING.

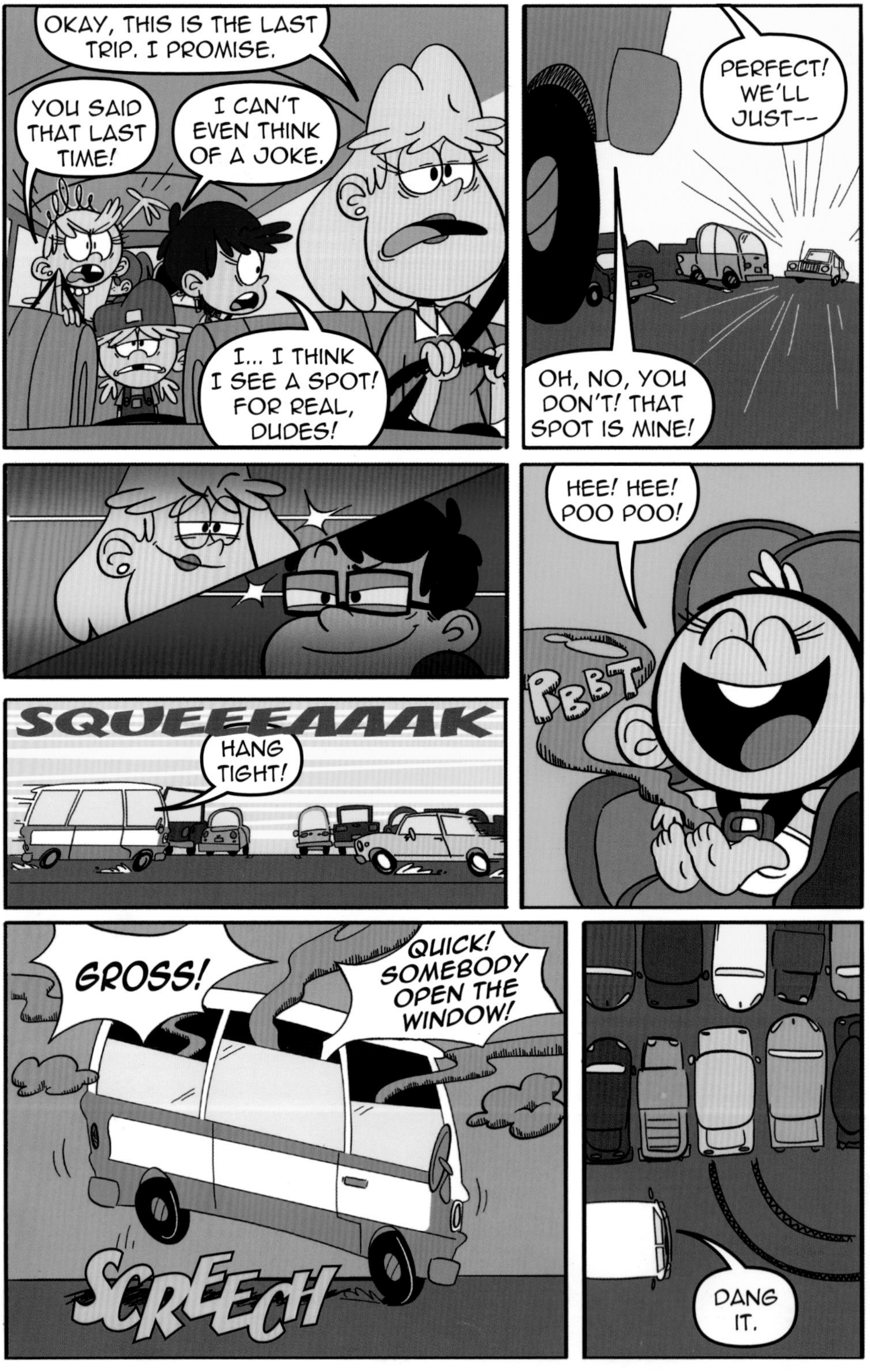

OKAY, THIS IS THE LAST TRIP. I PROMISE.
YOU SAID THAT LAST TIME!
I CAN'T EVEN THINK OF A JOKE.
I... I THINK I SEE A SPOT! FOR REAL, DUDES!
PERFECT! WE'LL JUST--
OH, NO, YOU DON'T! THAT SPOT IS MINE!
SQUEEEAAAK
HANG TIGHT!
HEE! HEE! POO POO!
PBBT
GROSS!
QUICK! SOMEBODY OPEN THE WINDOW!
SCREECH
DANG IT.

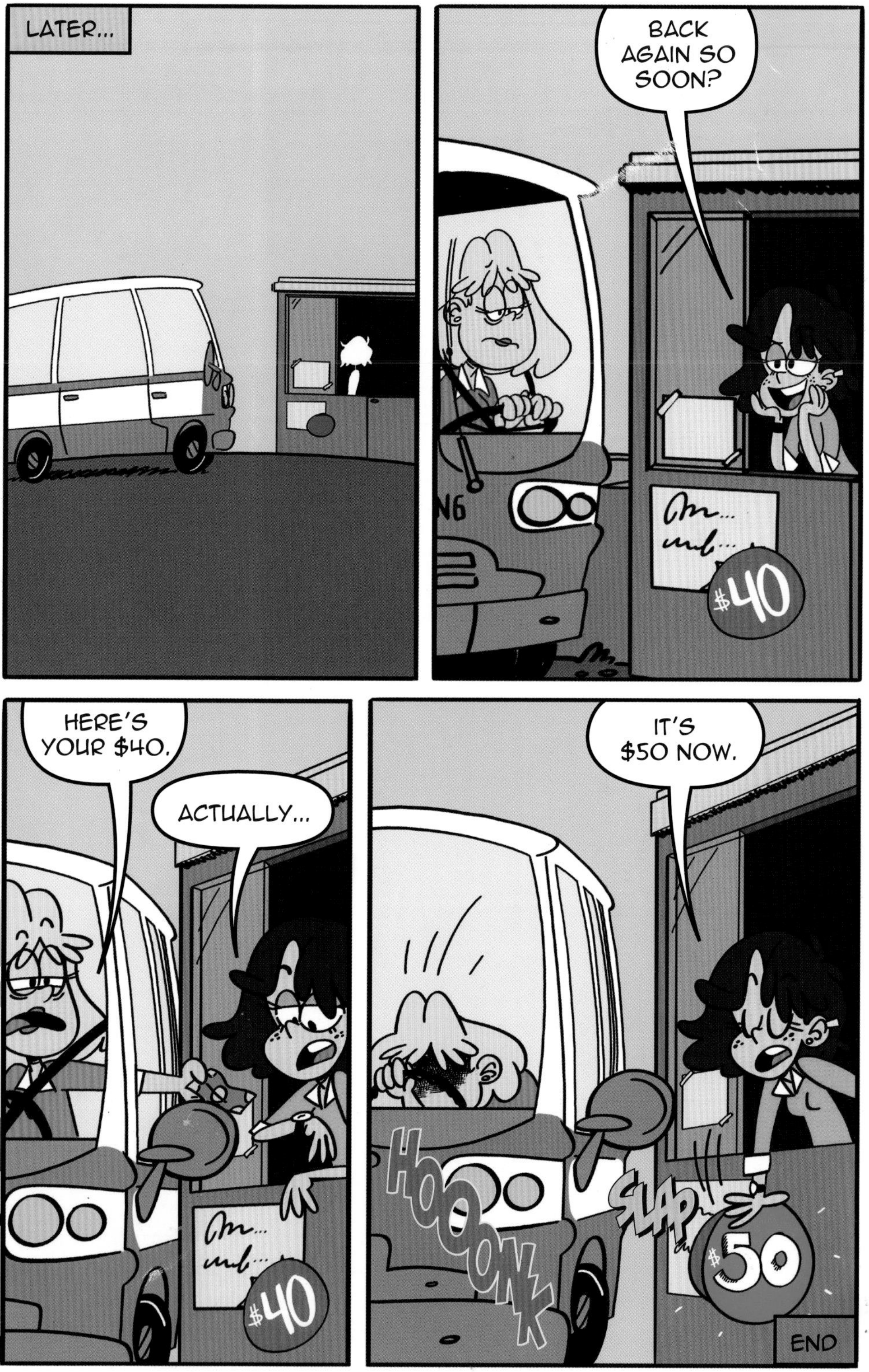

LATER...
BACK AGAIN SO SOON?
$40
HERE'S YOUR $40.
ACTUALLY...
$40
IT'S $50 NOW.
HOOOONK
SLAP
$50
END

"DIVIDE AND CONQUER"

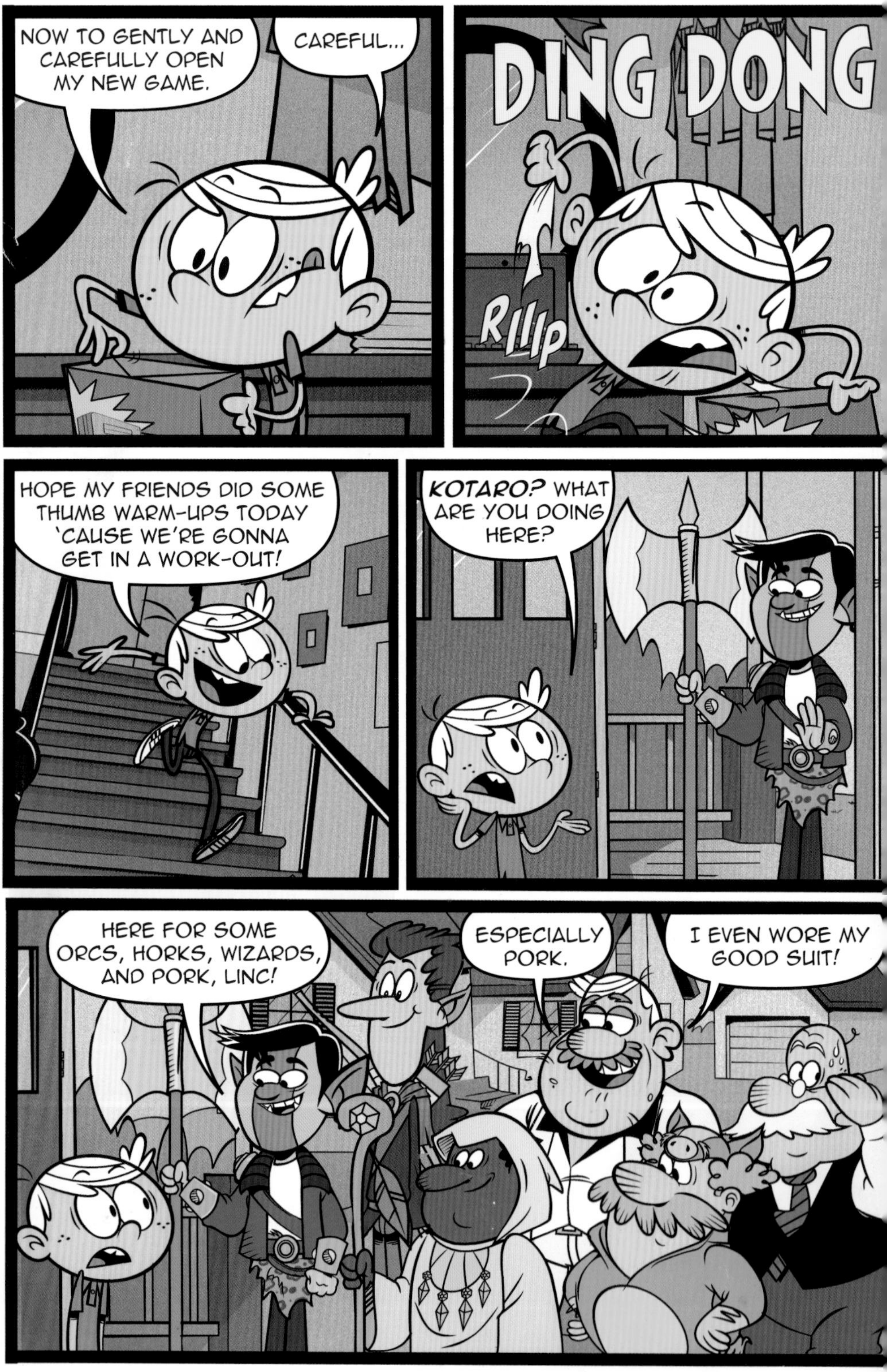
NOW TO GENTLY AND CAREFULLY OPEN MY NEW GAME.
CAREFUL...
DING DONG
RIIP
HOPE MY FRIENDS DID SOME THUMB WARM-UPS TODAY 'CAUSE WE'RE GONNA GET IN A WORK-OUT!
KOTARO? WHAT ARE YOU DOING HERE?
HERE FOR SOME ORCS, HORKS, WIZARDS, AND PORK, LINC!
ESPECIALLY PORK.
I EVEN WORE MY GOOD SUIT!

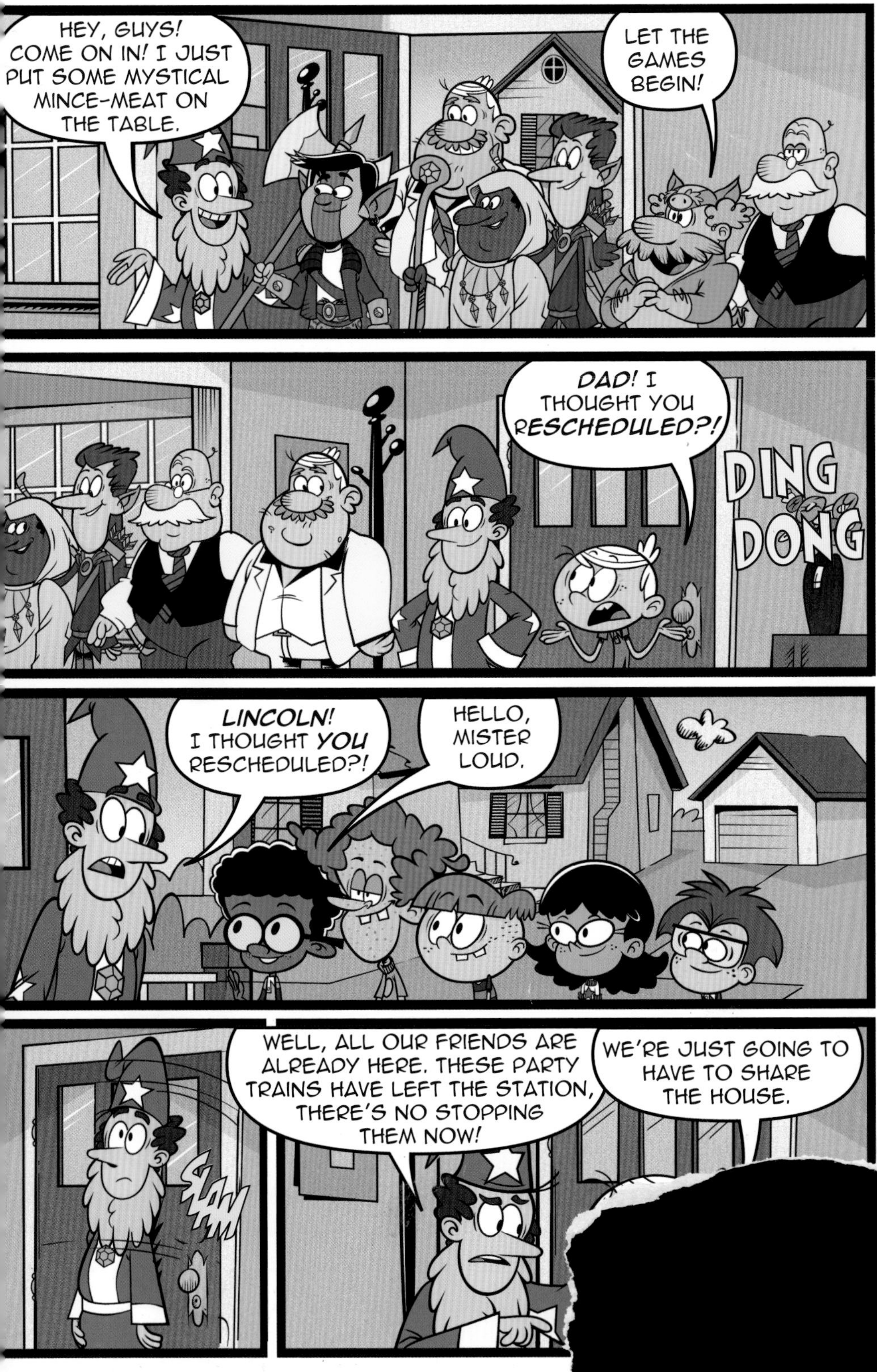
HEY, GUYS! COME ON IN! I JUST PUT SOME MYSTICAL MINCE-MEAT ON THE TABLE.
LET THE GAMES BEGIN!
DAD! I THOUGHT YOU RESCHEDULED?!
DING DONG
LINCOLN! I THOUGHT YOU RESCHEDULED?!
HELLO, MISTER LOUD.
SLAM
WELL, ALL OUR FRIENDS ARE ALREADY HERE. THESE PARTY TRAINS HAVE LEFT THE STATION, THERE'S NO STOPPING THEM NOW!
WE'RE JUST GOING TO HAVE TO SHARE THE HOUSE.

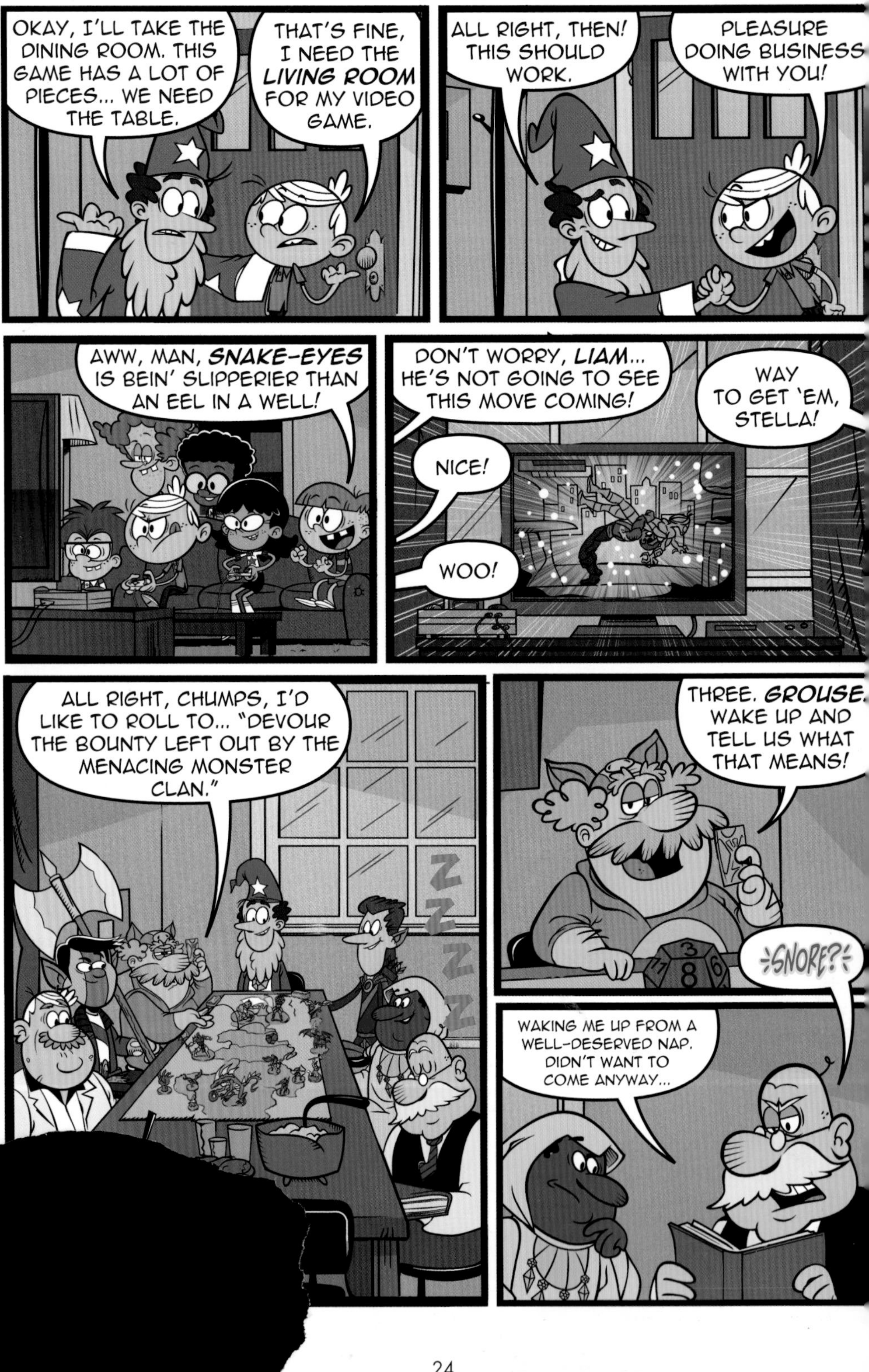

OKAY, I'LL TAKE THE DINING ROOM. THIS GAME HAS A LOT OF PIECES... WE NEED THE TABLE.
THAT'S FINE, I NEED THE LIVING ROOM FOR MY VIDEO GAME.
ALL RIGHT, THEN! THIS SHOULD WORK.
PLEASURE DOING BUSINESS WITH YOU!
AWW, MAN, SNAKE-EYES IS BEIN' SLIPPERIER THAN AN EEL IN A WELL!
DON'T WORRY, LIAM... HE'S NOT GOING TO SEE THIS MOVE COMING!
WAY TO GET 'EM, STELLA!
NICE!
WOO!
ALL RIGHT, CHUMPS, I'D LIKE TO ROLL TO... "DEVOUR THE BOUNTY LEFT OUT BY THE MENACING MONSTER CLAN."
THREE. GROUSE. WAKE UP AND TELL US WHAT THAT MEANS!
SNORE?
WAKING ME UP FROM A WELL-DESERVED NAP. DIDN'T WANT TO COME ANYWAY...

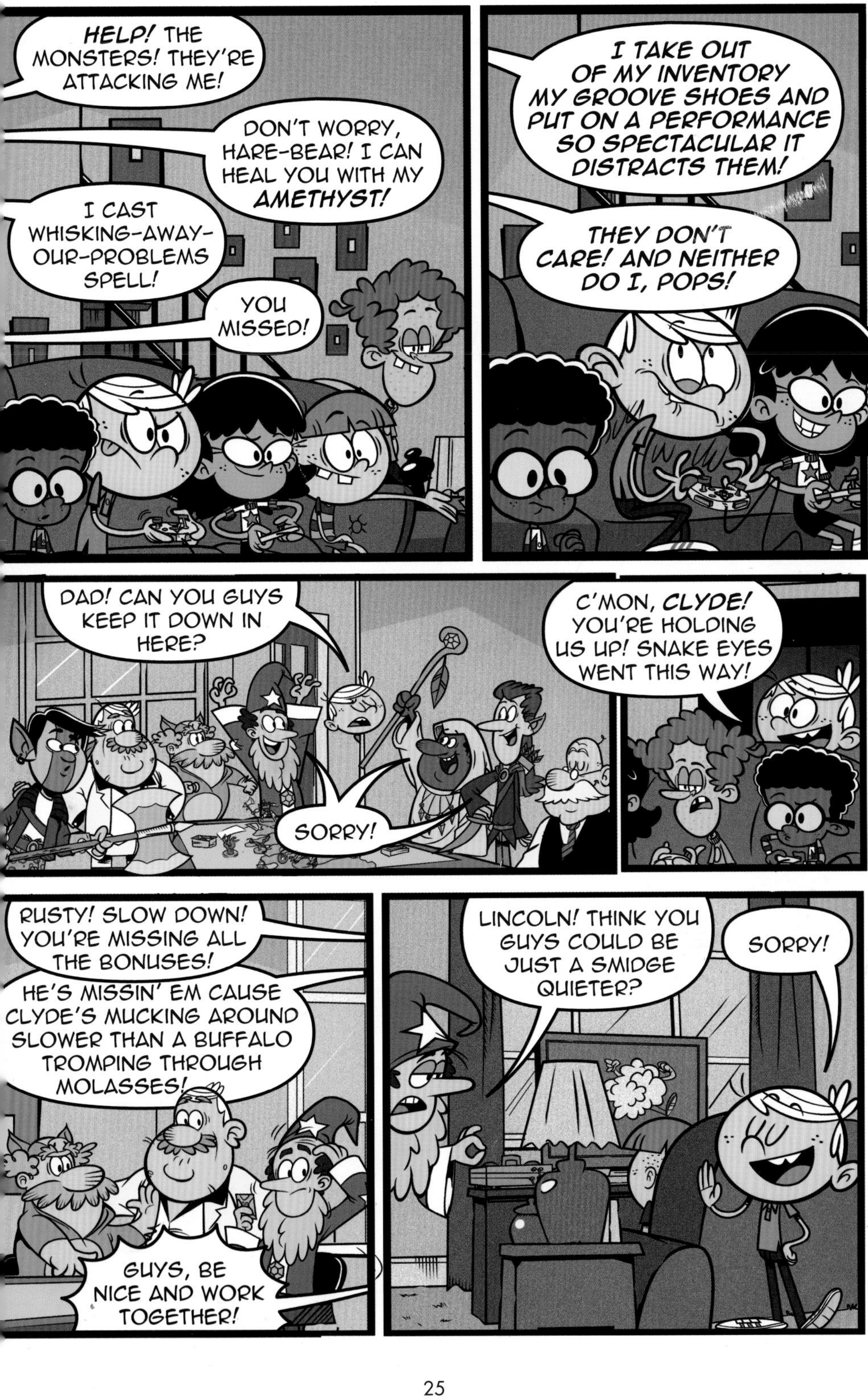
HELP! THE MONSTERS! THEY'RE ATTACKING ME!
DON'T WORRY, HARE-BEAR! I CAN HEAL YOU WITH MY AMETHYST!
I CAST WHISKING-AWAY-OUR-PROBLEMS SPELL!
YOU MISSED!
I TAKE OUT OF MY INVENTORY MY GROOVE SHOES AND PUT ON A PERFORMANCE SO SPECTACULAR IT DISTRACTS THEM!
THEY DON'T CARE! AND NEITHER DO I, POPS!
DAD! CAN YOU GUYS KEEP IT DOWN IN HERE?
SORRY!
C'MON, CLYDE! YOU'RE HOLDING US UP! SNAKE EYES WENT THIS WAY!
RUSTY! SLOW DOWN! YOU'RE MISSING ALL THE BONUSES!
HE'S MISSIN' EM CAUSE CLYDE'S MUCKING AROUND SLOWER THAN A BUFFALO TROMPING THROUGH MOLASSES!
GUYS, BE NICE AND WORK TOGETHER!
LINCOLN! THINK YOU GUYS COULD BE JUST A SMIDGE QUIETER?
SORRY!

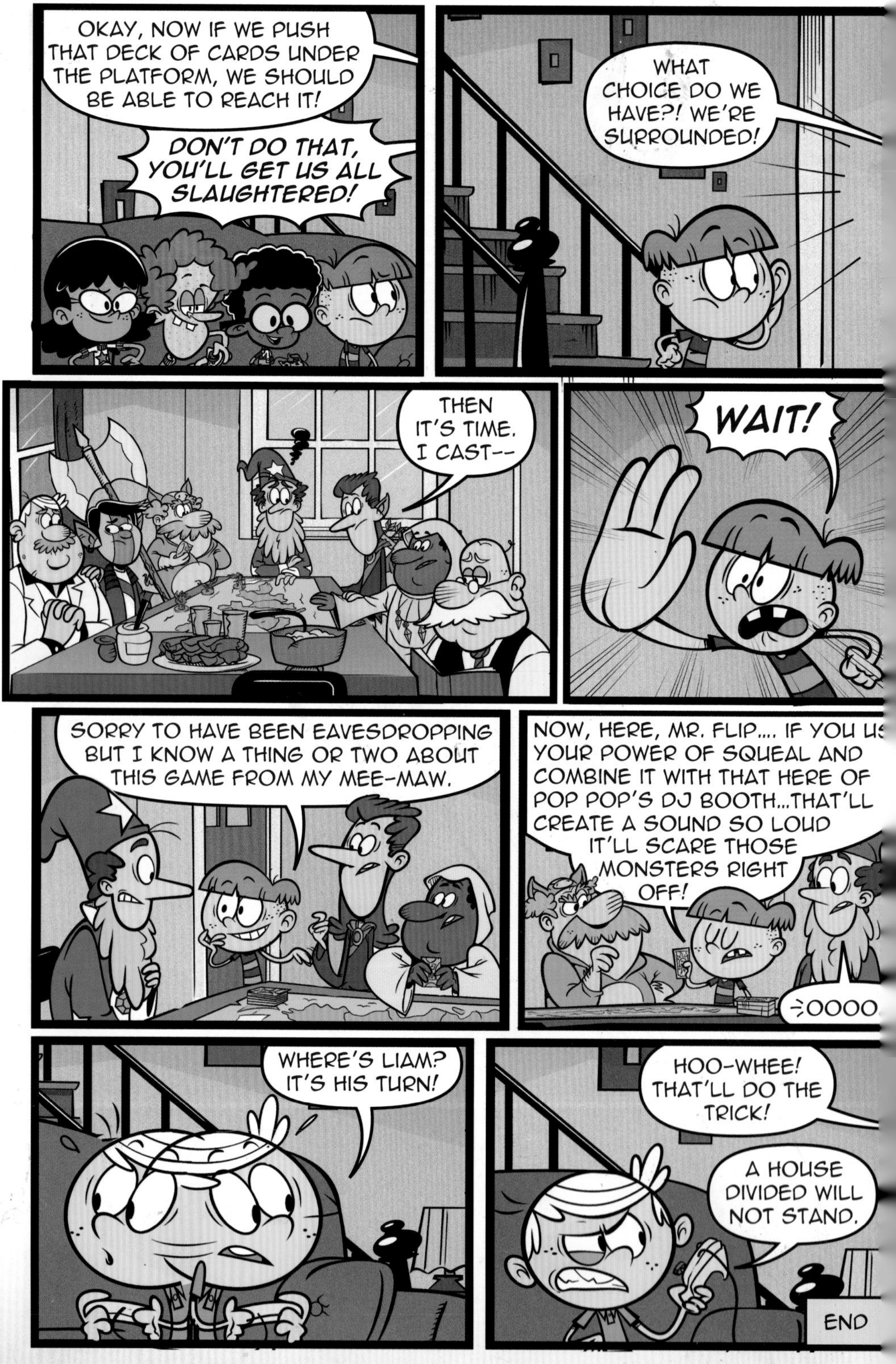
OKAY, NOW IF WE PUSH THAT DECK OF CARDS UNDER THE PLATFORM, WE SHOULD BE ABLE TO REACH IT!
DON'T DO THAT, YOU'LL GET US ALL SLAUGHTERED!
WHAT CHOICE DO WE HAVE?! WE'RE SURROUNDED!
THEN IT'S TIME. I CAST--
WAIT!
SORRY TO HAVE BEEN EAVESDROPPING BUT I KNOW A THING OR TWO ABOUT THIS GAME FROM MY MEE-MAW.
NOW, HERE, MR. FLIP.... IF YOU US YOUR POWER OF SQUEAL AND COMBINE IT WITH THAT HERE OF POP POP'S DJ BOOTH...THAT'LL CREATE A SOUND SO LOUD IT'LL SCARE THOSE MONSTERS RIGHT OFF!
OOOO
WHERE'S LIAM? IT'S HIS TURN!
HOO-WHEE! THAT'LL DO THE TRICK!
A HOUSE DIVIDED WILL NOT STAND.
END

"HAGGLE TALE"

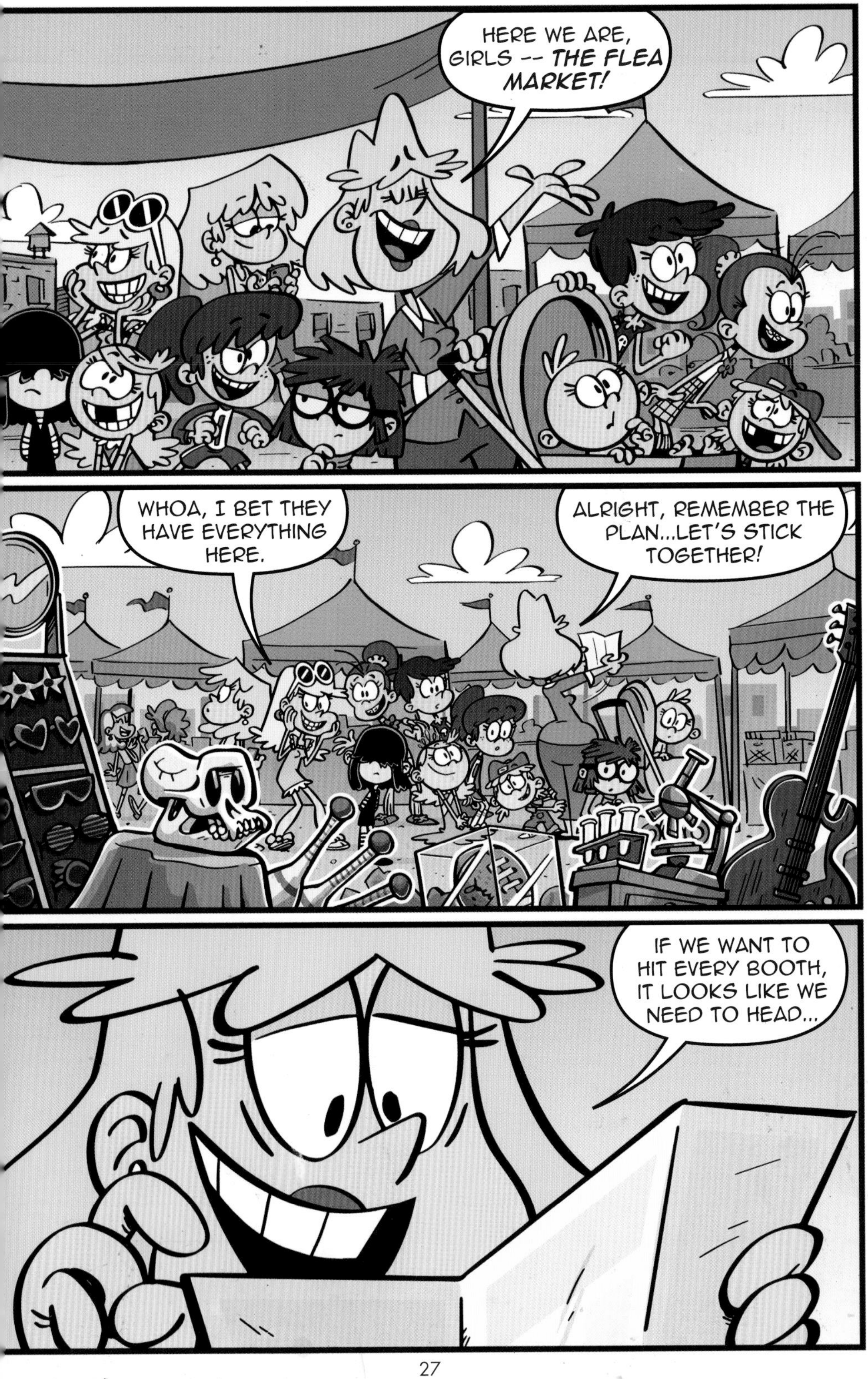

HERE WE ARE, GIRLS -- THE FLEA MARKET!
WHOA, I BET THEY HAVE EVERYTHING HERE.
ALRIGHT, REMEMBER THE PLAN...LET'S STICK TOGETHER!
IF WE WANT TO HIT EVERY BOOTH, IT LOOKS LIKE WE NEED TO HEAD...

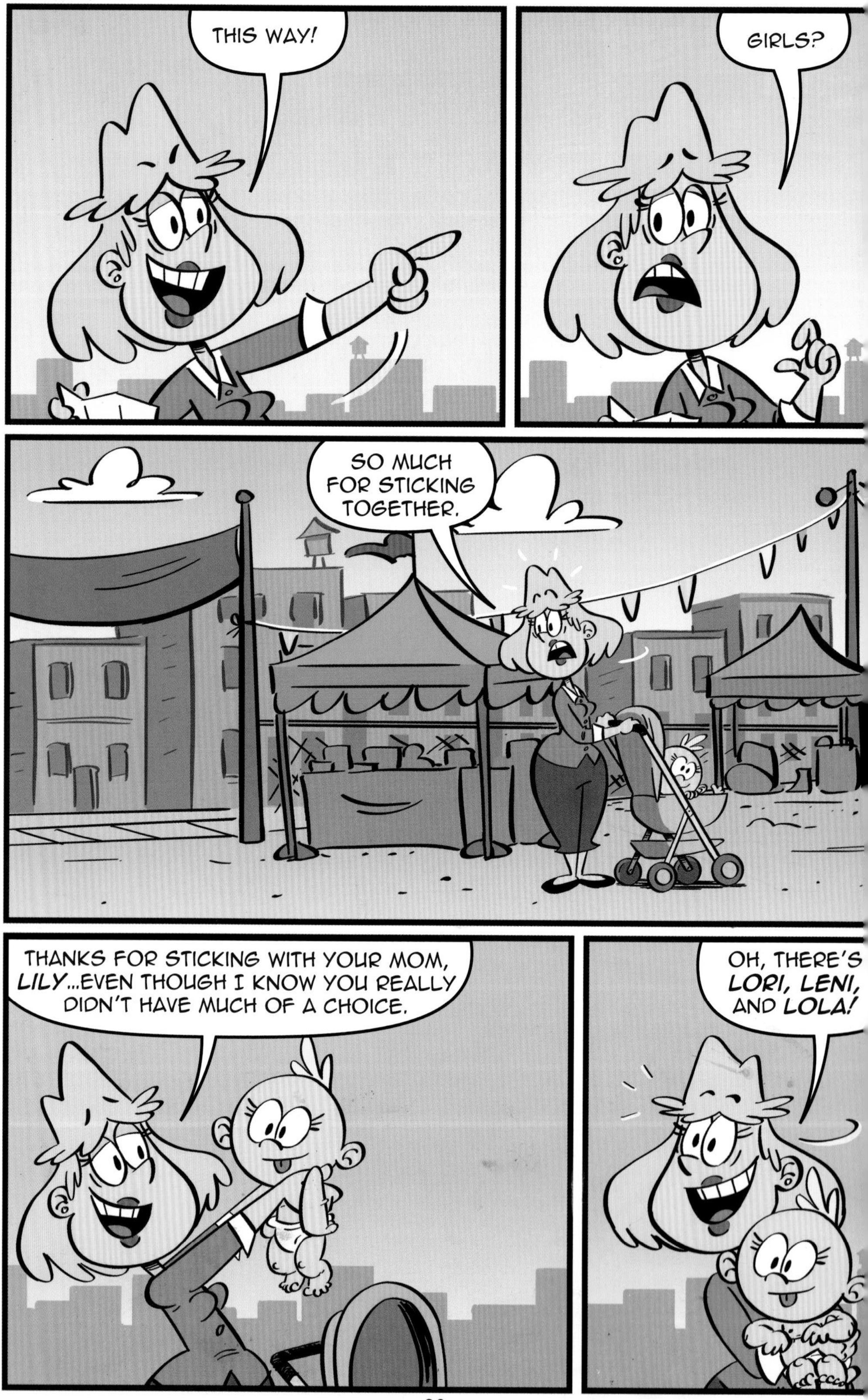
THIS WAY!
GIRLS?
SO MUCH FOR STICKING TOGETHER.
THANKS FOR STICKING WITH YOUR MOM, LILY...EVEN THOUGH I KNOW YOU REALLY DIDN'T HAVE MUCH OF A CHOICE.
OH, THERE'S LORI, LENI, AND LOLA!

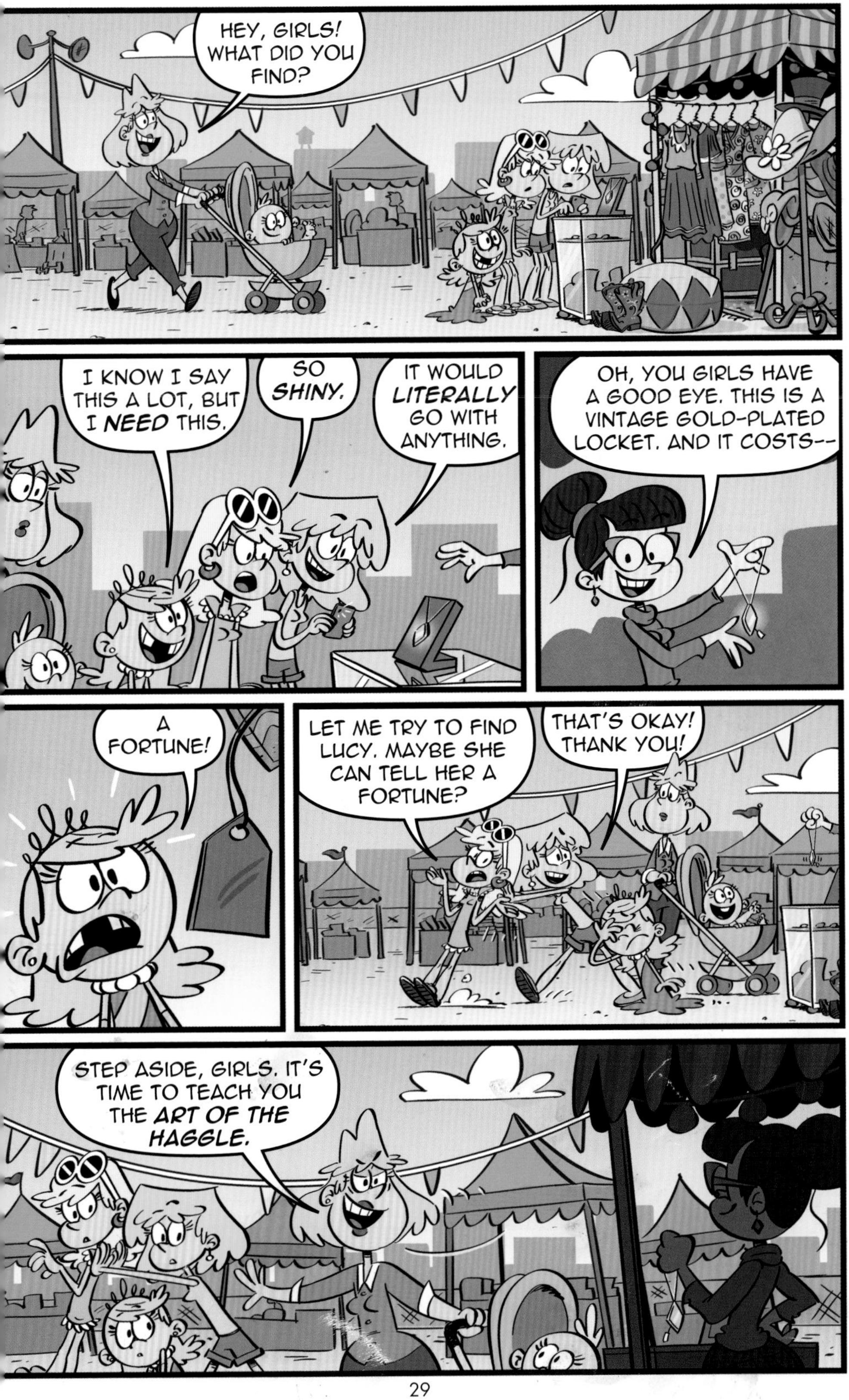
HEY, GIRLS! WHAT DID YOU FIND?
I KNOW I SAY THIS A LOT, BUT I NEED THIS.
SO SHINY.
IT WOULD LITERALLY GO WITH ANYTHING.
OH, YOU GIRLS HAVE A GOOD EYE. THIS IS A VINTAGE GOLD-PLATED LOCKET. AND IT COSTS--
A FORTUNE!
LET ME TRY TO FIND LUCY. MAYBE SHE CAN TELL HER A FORTUNE?
THAT'S OKAY! THANK YOU!
STEP ASIDE, GIRLS. IT'S TIME TO TEACH YOU THE ART OF THE HAGGLE.

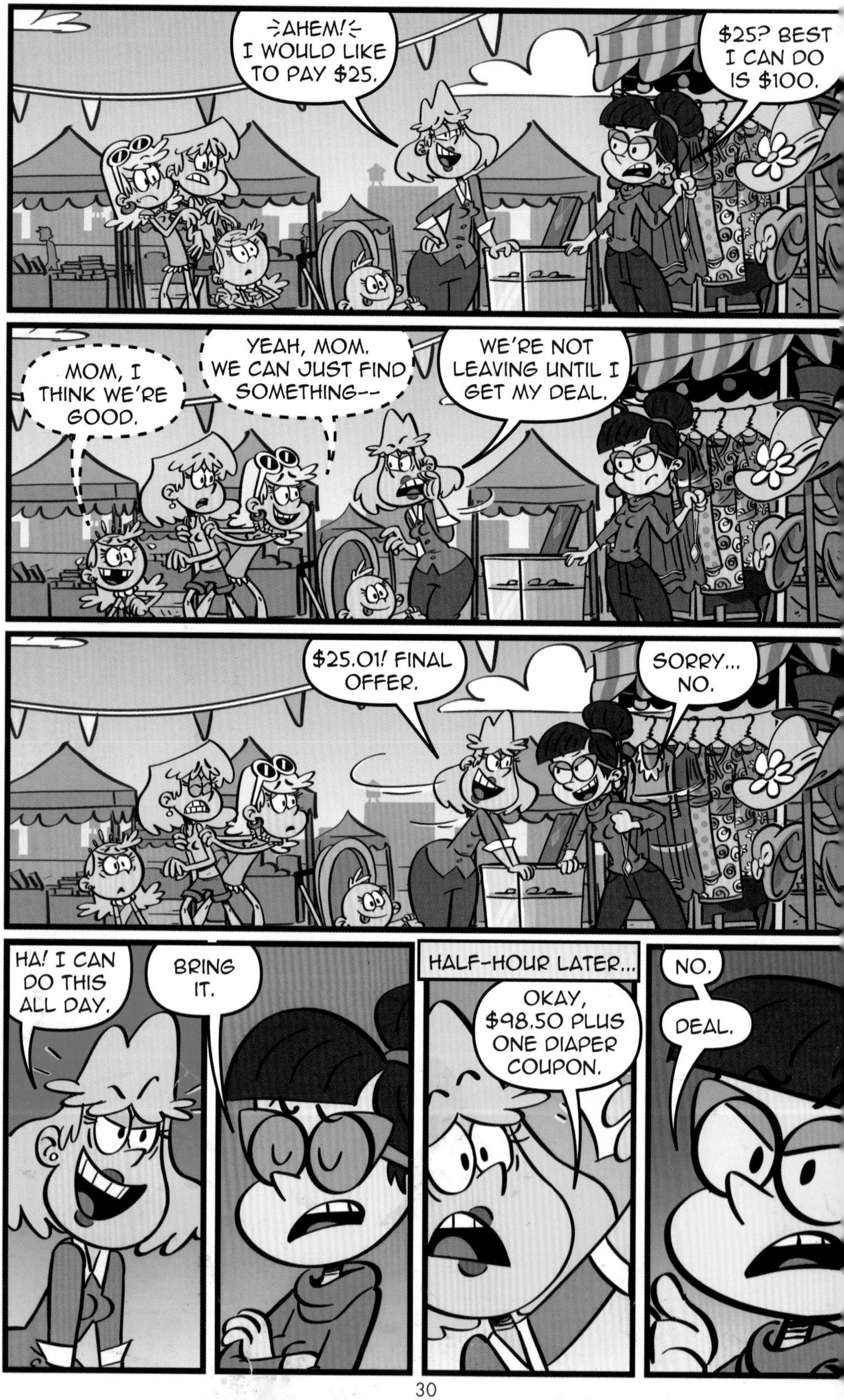
AHEM! I WOULD LIKE TO PAY $25.
$25? BEST I CAN DO IS $100.
MOM, I THINK WE'RE GOOD.
YEAH, MOM. WE CAN JUST FIND SOMETHING--
WE'RE NOT LEAVING UNTIL I GET MY DEAL.
$25.01! FINAL OFFER.
SORRY... NO.
HA! I CAN DO THIS ALL DAY.
BRING IT.
HALF-HOUR LATER...
OKAY, $98.50 PLUS ONE DIAPER COUPON.
NO.
DEAL.

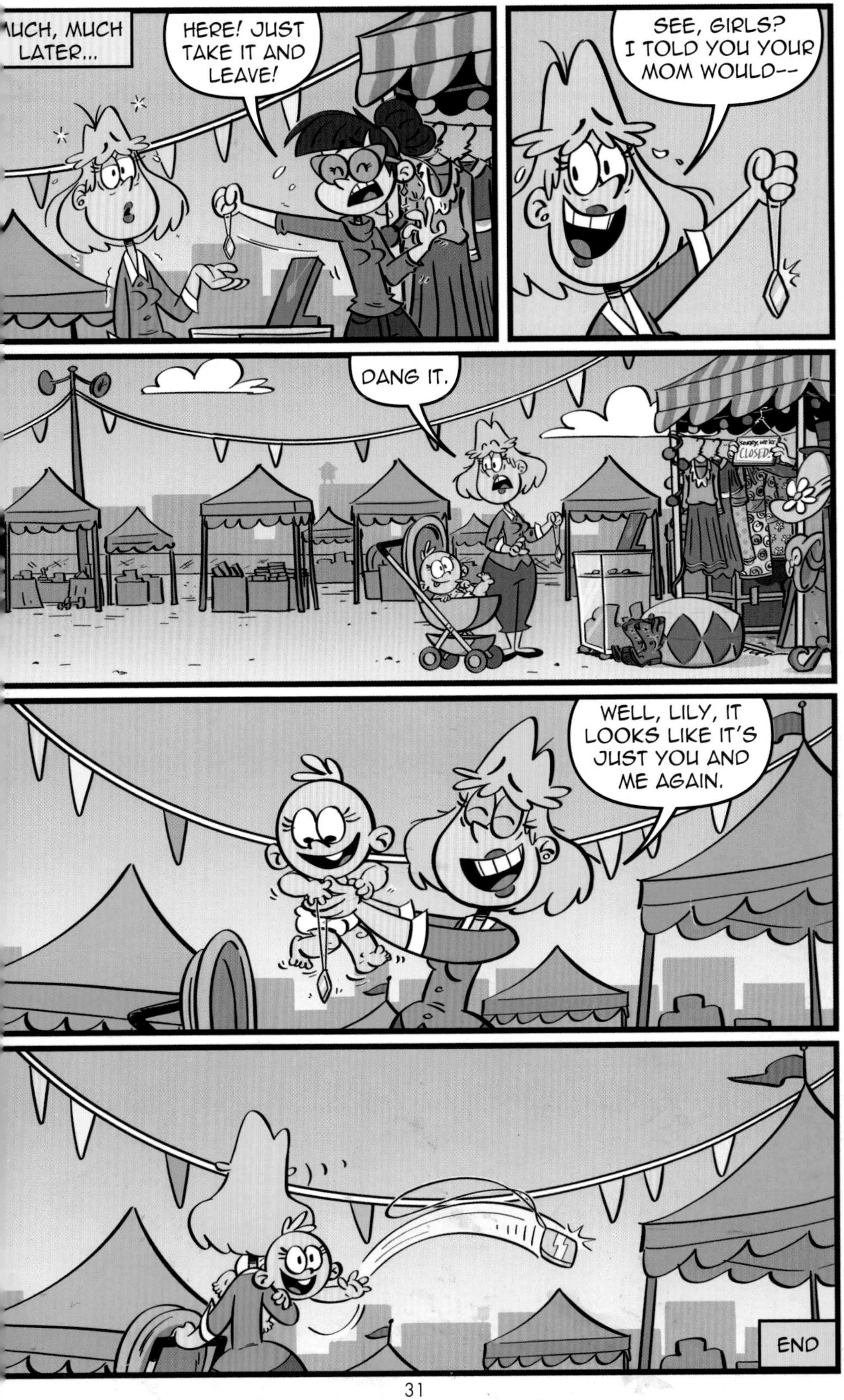
MUCH, MUCH LATER...
HERE! JUST TAKE IT AND LEAVE!
SEE, GIRLS? I TOLD YOU YOUR MOM WOULD--
DANG IT.
CLOSED
WELL, LILY, IT LOOKS LIKE IT'S JUST YOU AND ME AGAIN.
END

"PARTY HOPPERS"

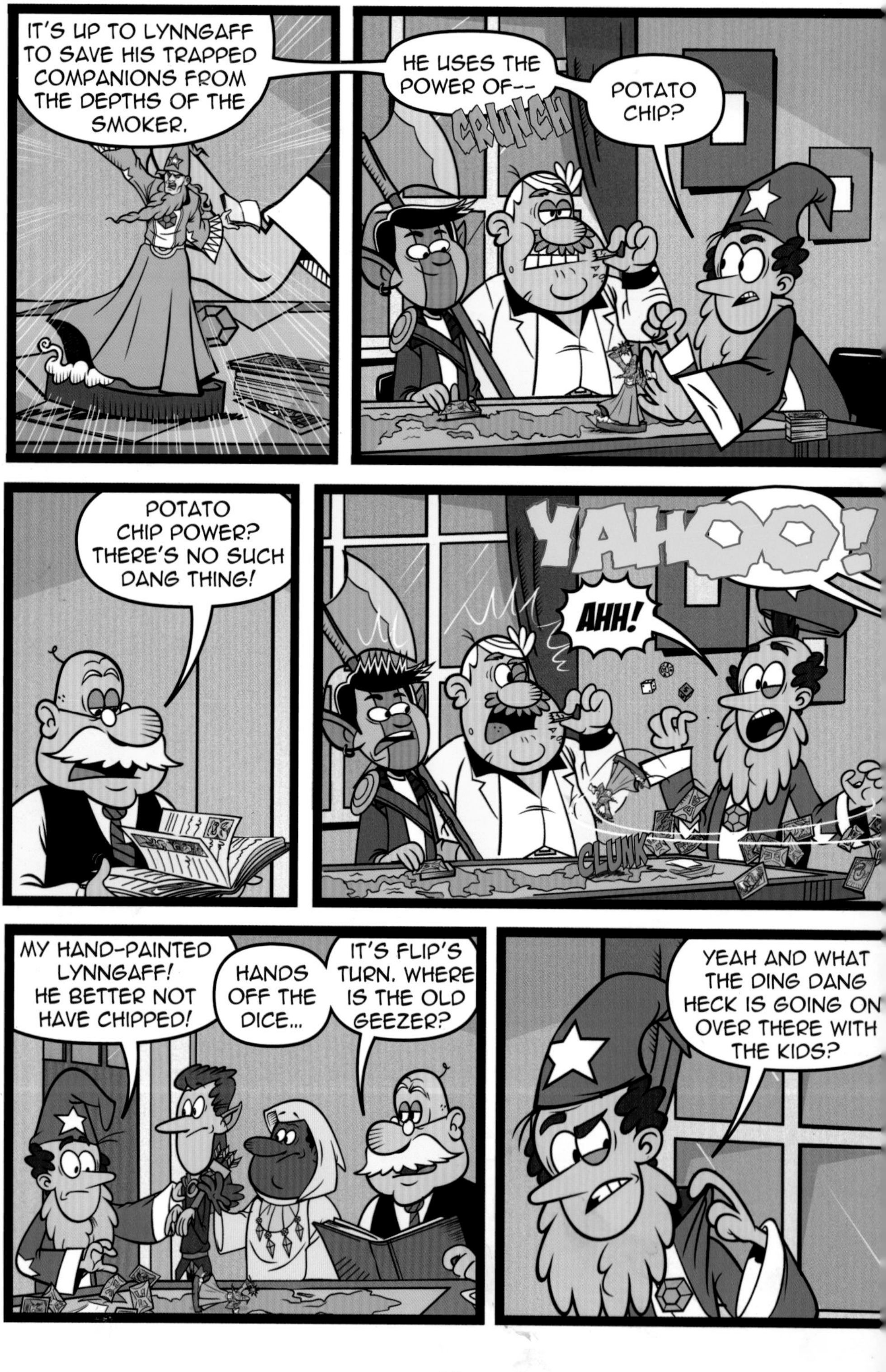
IT'S UP TO LYNNGAFF TO SAVE HIS TRAPPED COMPANIONS FROM THE DEPTHS OF THE SMOKER.
HE USES THE POWER OF--
CRUNCH
POTATO CHIP?
POTATO CHIP POWER? THERE'S NO SUCH DANG THING!
YAHOO!
AHH!
CLUNK
MY HAND-PAINTED LYNNGAFF! HE BETTER NOT HAVE CHIPPED!
HANDS OFF THE DICE...
IT'S FLIP'S TURN. WHERE IS THE OLD GEEZER?
YEAH AND WHAT THE DING DANG HECK IS GOING ON OVER THERE WITH THE KIDS?

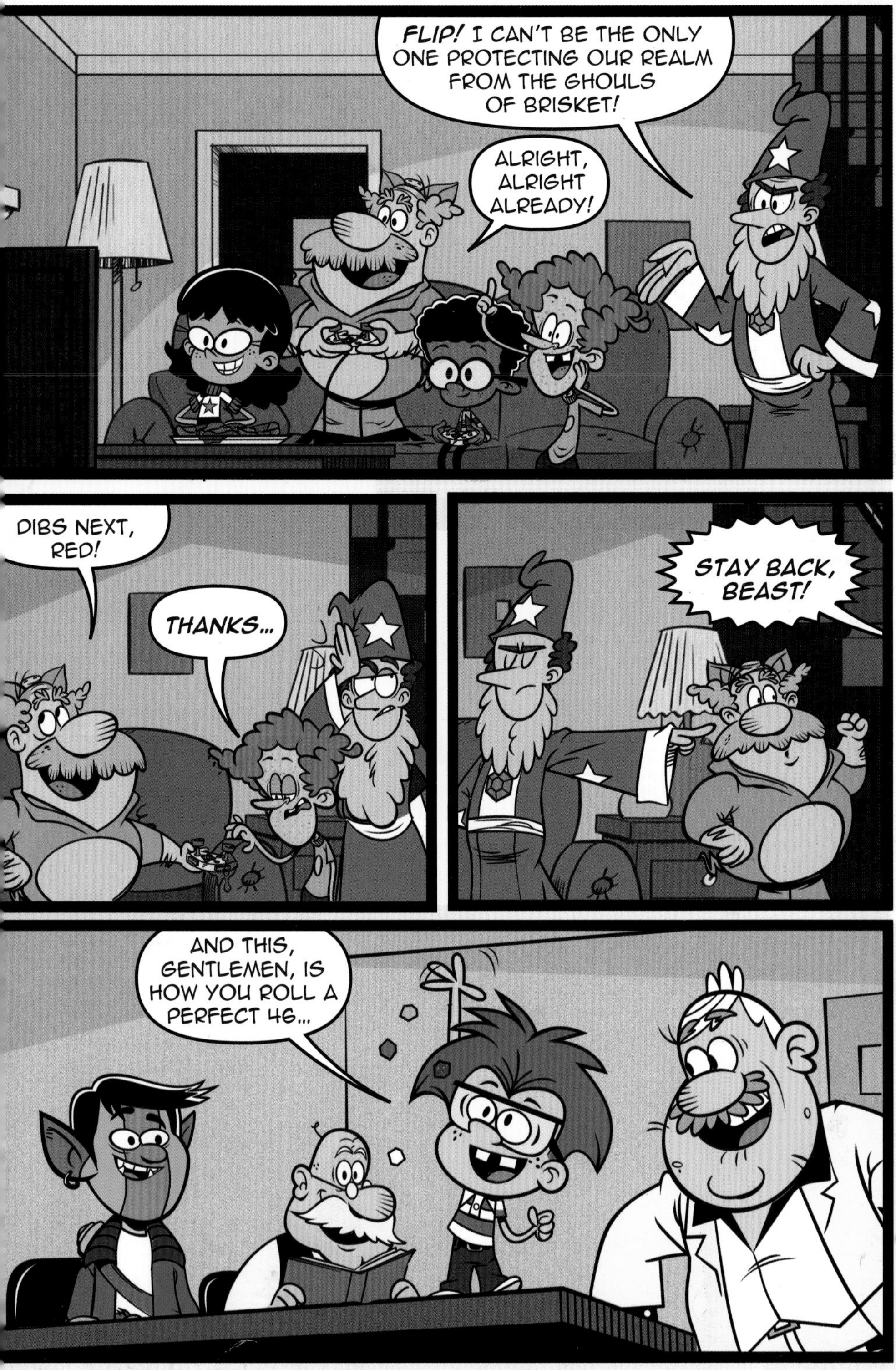
FLIP! I CAN'T BE THE ONLY ONE PROTECTING OUR REALM FROM THE GHOULS OF BRISKET!
ALRIGHT, ALRIGHT ALREADY!
DIBS NEXT, RED!
THANKS...
STAY BACK, BEAST!
AND THIS, GENTLEMEN, IS HOW YOU ROLL A PERFECT 46...

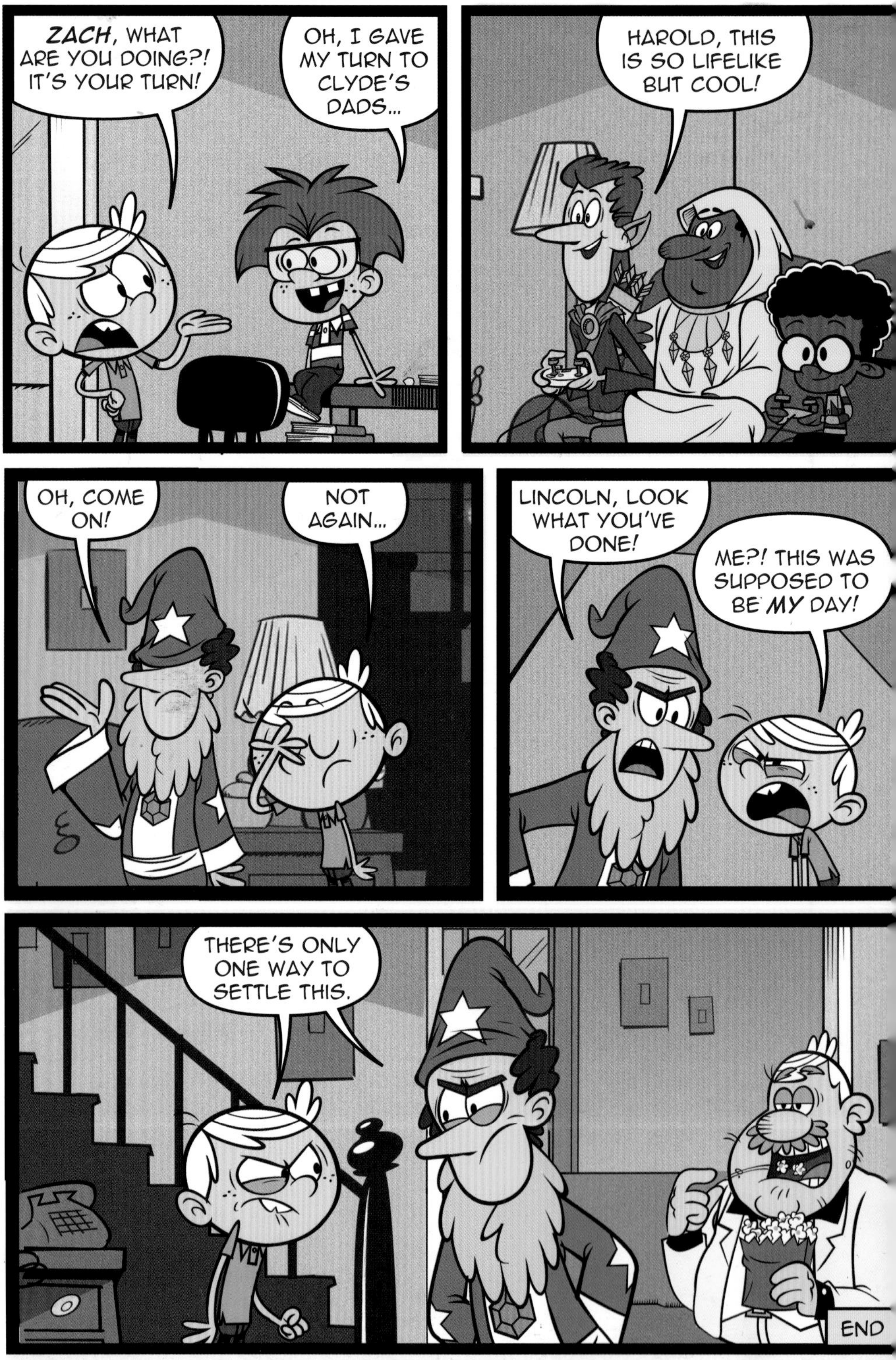
ZACH, WHAT ARE YOU DOING?! IT'S YOUR TURN!
OH, I GAVE MY TURN TO CLYDE'S DADS...
HAROLD, THIS IS SO LIFELIKE BUT COOL!
OH, COME ON!
NOT AGAIN...
LINCOLN, LOOK WHAT YOU'VE DONE!
ME?! THIS WAS SUPPOSED TO BE MY DAY!
THERE'S ONLY ONE WAY TO SETTLE THIS.
END

"THE FLEA MARKET"

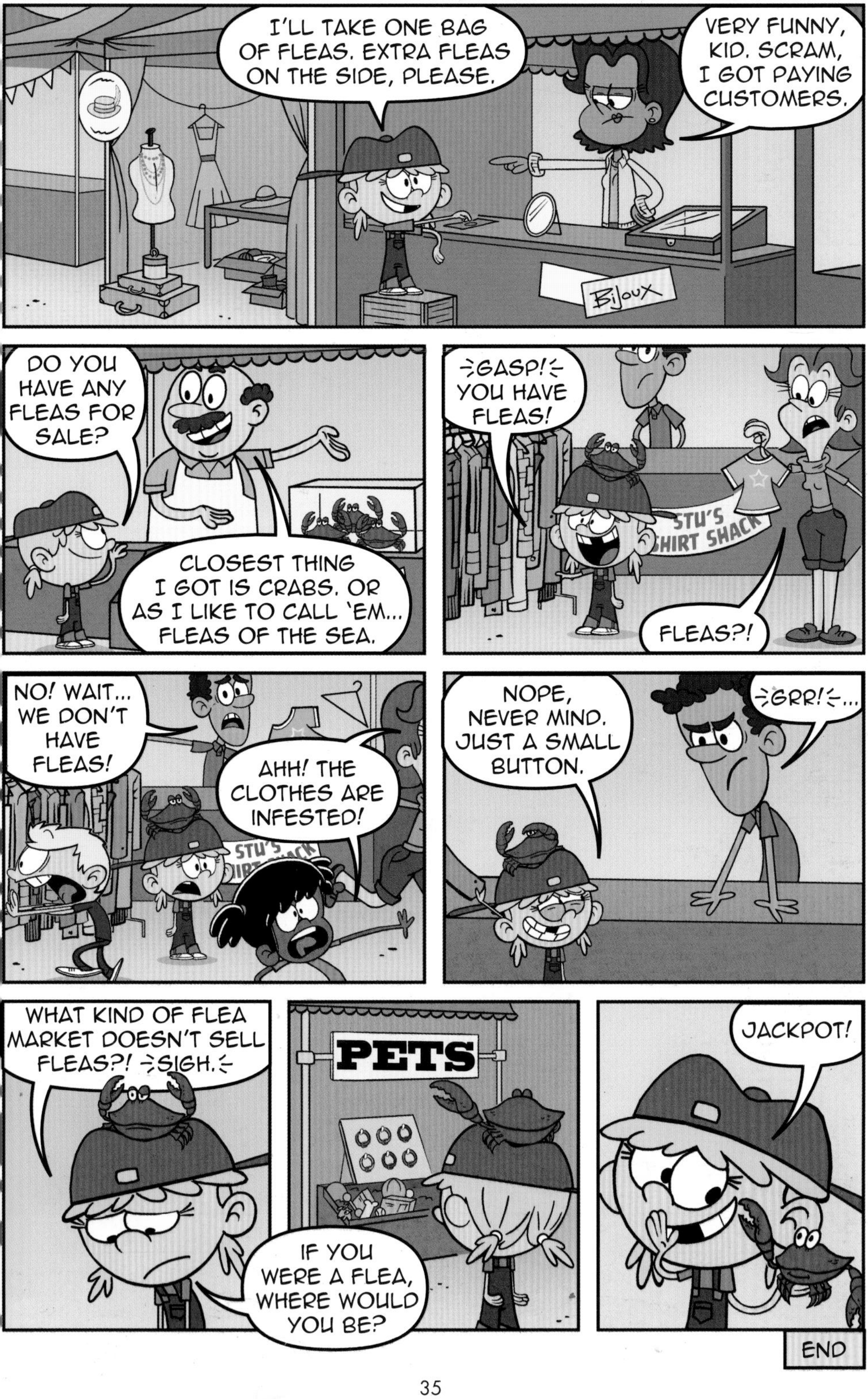

I'LL TAKE ONE BAG OF FLEAS. EXTRA FLEAS ON THE SIDE, PLEASE.
VERY FUNNY, KID. SCRAM, I GOT PAYING CUSTOMERS.
BIJOUX
DO YOU HAVE ANY FLEAS FOR SALE?
CLOSEST THING I GOT IS CRABS. OR AS I LIKE TO CALL 'EM... FLEAS OF THE SEA.
GASP! YOU HAVE FLEAS!
STU'S SHIRT SHACK
FLEAS?!
NO! WAIT... WE DON'T HAVE FLEAS!
AHH! THE CLOTHES ARE INFESTED!
NOPE, NEVER MIND. JUST A SMALL BUTTON.
GRR!...
WHAT KIND OF FLEA MARKET DOESN'T SELL FLEAS?! SIGH.
PETS
IF YOU WERE A FLEA, WHERE WOULD YOU BE?
JACKPOT!
END

"RACE TO THE THRONE"

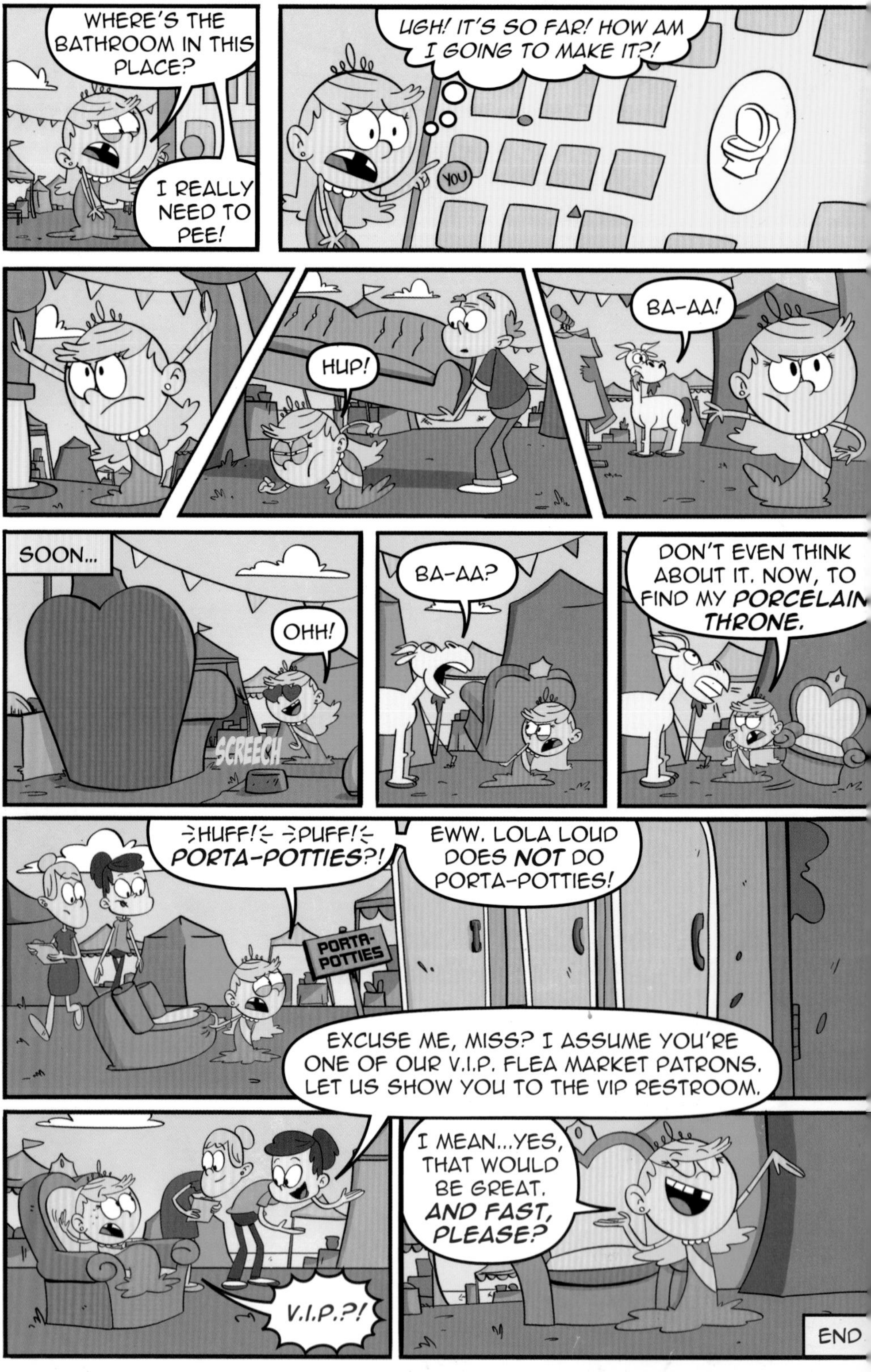
WHERE'S THE BATHROOM IN THIS PLACE?
I REALLY NEED TO PEE!
UGH! IT'S SO FAR! HOW AM I GOING TO MAKE IT?!
YOU
HUP!
BA-AA!
SOON...
OHH!
SCREECH
BA-AA?
DON'T EVEN THINK ABOUT IT. NOW, TO FIND MY *PORCELAIN THRONE.*
HUFF! PUFF! *PORTA-POTTIES?!*
EWW. LOLA LOUD DOES **NOT** DO PORTA-POTTIES!
PORTA-POTTIES
EXCUSE ME, MISS? I ASSUME YOU'RE ONE OF OUR V.I.P. FLEA MARKET PATRONS. LET US SHOW YOU TO THE VIP RESTROOM.
V.I.P.?!
I MEAN...YES, THAT WOULD BE GREAT. *AND FAST, PLEASE?*
END

"RECORD TIME"

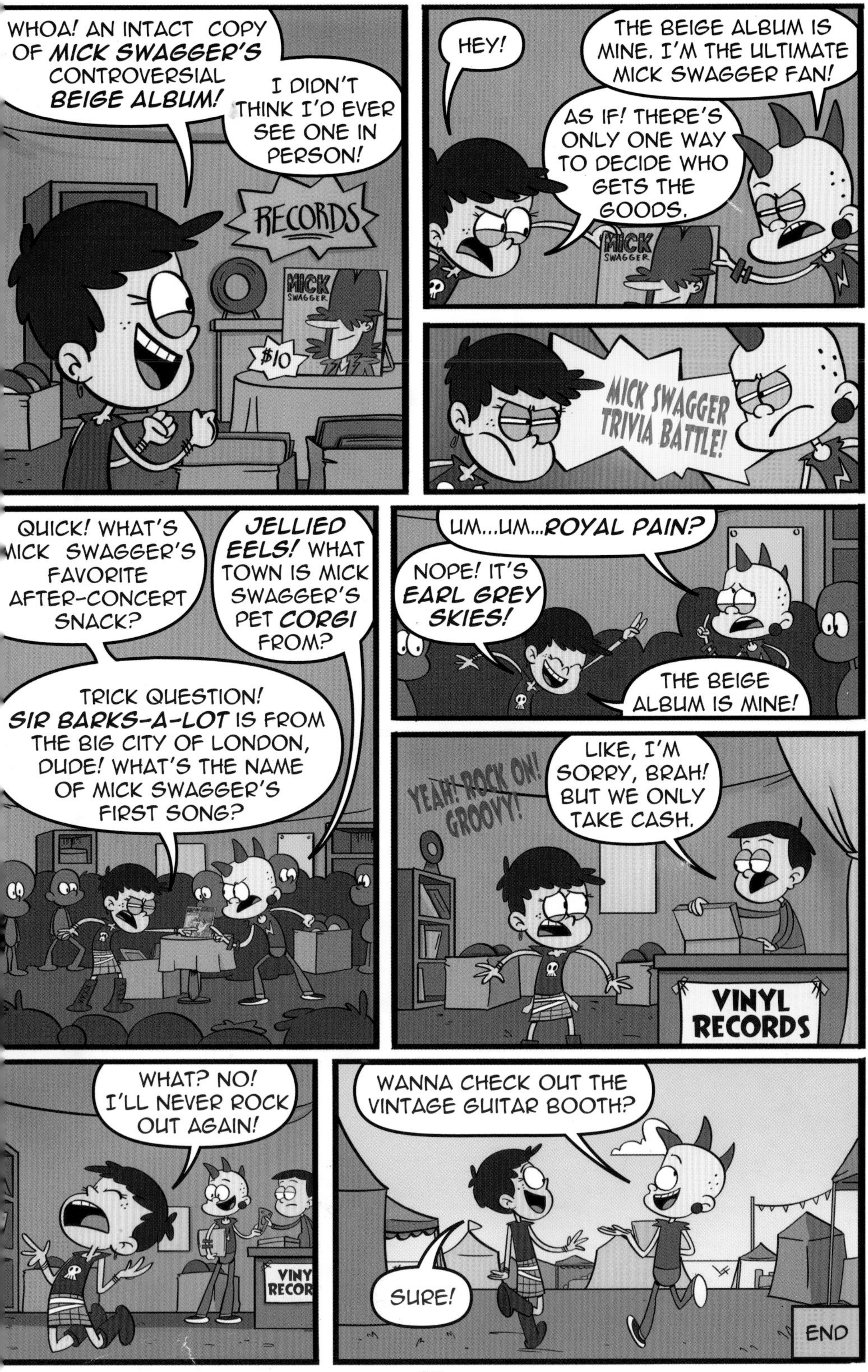
WHOA! AN INTACT COPY OF MICK SWAGGER'S CONTROVERSIAL BEIGE ALBUM!
I DIDN'T THINK I'D EVER SEE ONE IN PERSON!
RECORDS
MICK SWAGGER
$10
HEY!
THE BEIGE ALBUM IS MINE. I'M THE ULTIMATE MICK SWAGGER FAN!
AS IF! THERE'S ONLY ONE WAY TO DECIDE WHO GETS THE GOODS.
MICK SWAGGER
MICK SWAGGER TRIVIA BATTLE!
QUICK! WHAT'S MICK SWAGGER'S FAVORITE AFTER-CONCERT SNACK?
JELLIED EELS! WHAT TOWN IS MICK SWAGGER'S PET CORGI FROM?
TRICK QUESTION! SIR BARKS-A-LOT IS FROM THE BIG CITY OF LONDON, DUDE! WHAT'S THE NAME OF MICK SWAGGER'S FIRST SONG?
UM...UM...ROYAL PAIN?
NOPE! IT'S EARL GREY SKIES!
THE BEIGE ALBUM IS MINE!
YEAH! ROCK ON! GROOVY!
LIKE, I'M SORRY, BRAH! BUT WE ONLY TAKE CASH.
VINYL RECORDS
WHAT? NO! I'LL NEVER ROCK OUT AGAIN!
WANNA CHECK OUT THE VINTAGE GUITAR BOOTH?
SURE!
END

"THE SAUCY LINE"

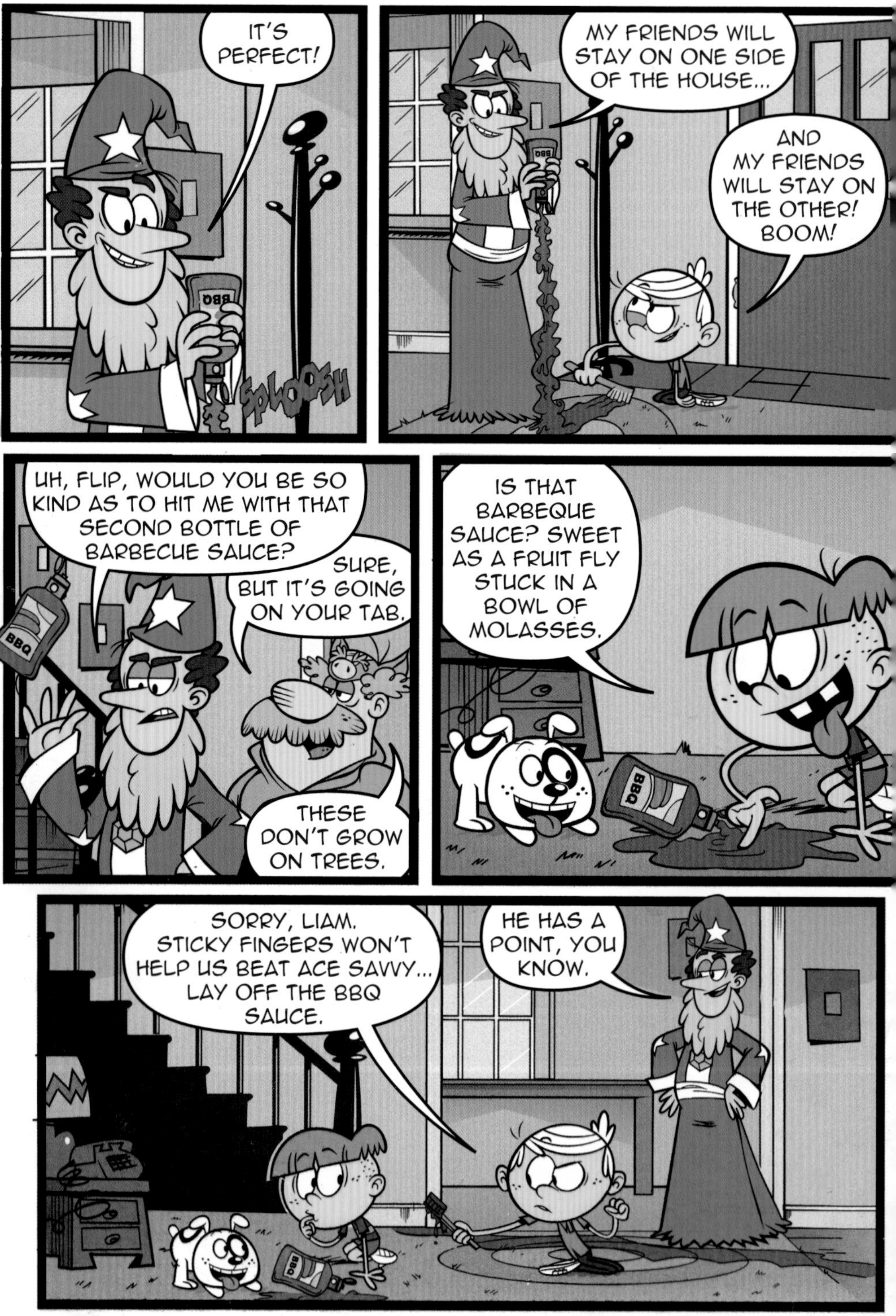
IT'S PERFECT!
SPLOOSH
MY FRIENDS WILL STAY ON ONE SIDE OF THE HOUSE...
AND MY FRIENDS WILL STAY ON THE OTHER! BOOM!
UH, FLIP, WOULD YOU BE SO KIND AS TO HIT ME WITH THAT SECOND BOTTLE OF BARBECUE SAUCE?
SURE, BUT IT'S GOING ON YOUR TAB.
THESE DON'T GROW ON TREES.
IS THAT BARBEQUE SAUCE? SWEET AS A FRUIT FLY STUCK IN A BOWL OF MOLASSES.
SORRY, LIAM. STICKY FINGERS WON'T HELP US BEAT ACE SAVVY... LAY OFF THE BBQ SAUCE.
HE HAS A POINT, YOU KNOW.

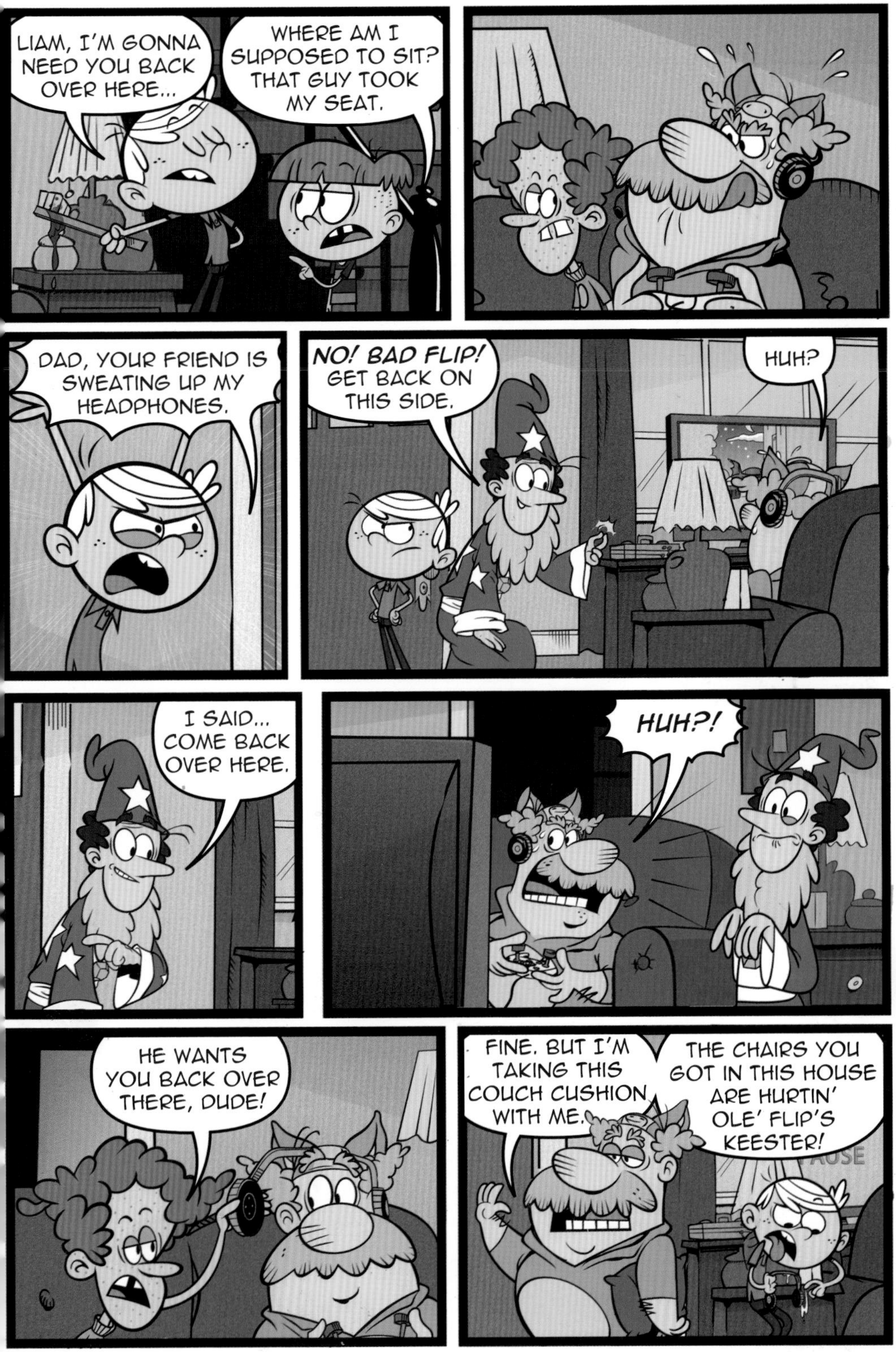
LIAM, I'M GONNA NEED YOU BACK OVER HERE...
WHERE AM I SUPPOSED TO SIT? THAT GUY TOOK MY SEAT.
DAD, YOUR FRIEND IS SWEATING UP MY HEADPHONES.
NO! BAD FLIP! GET BACK ON THIS SIDE.
HUH?
I SAID... COME BACK OVER HERE.
HUH?!
HE WANTS YOU BACK OVER THERE, DUDE!
FINE. BUT I'M TAKING THIS COUCH CUSHION WITH ME.
THE CHAIRS YOU GOT IN THIS HOUSE ARE HURTIN' OLE' FLIP'S KEESTER!

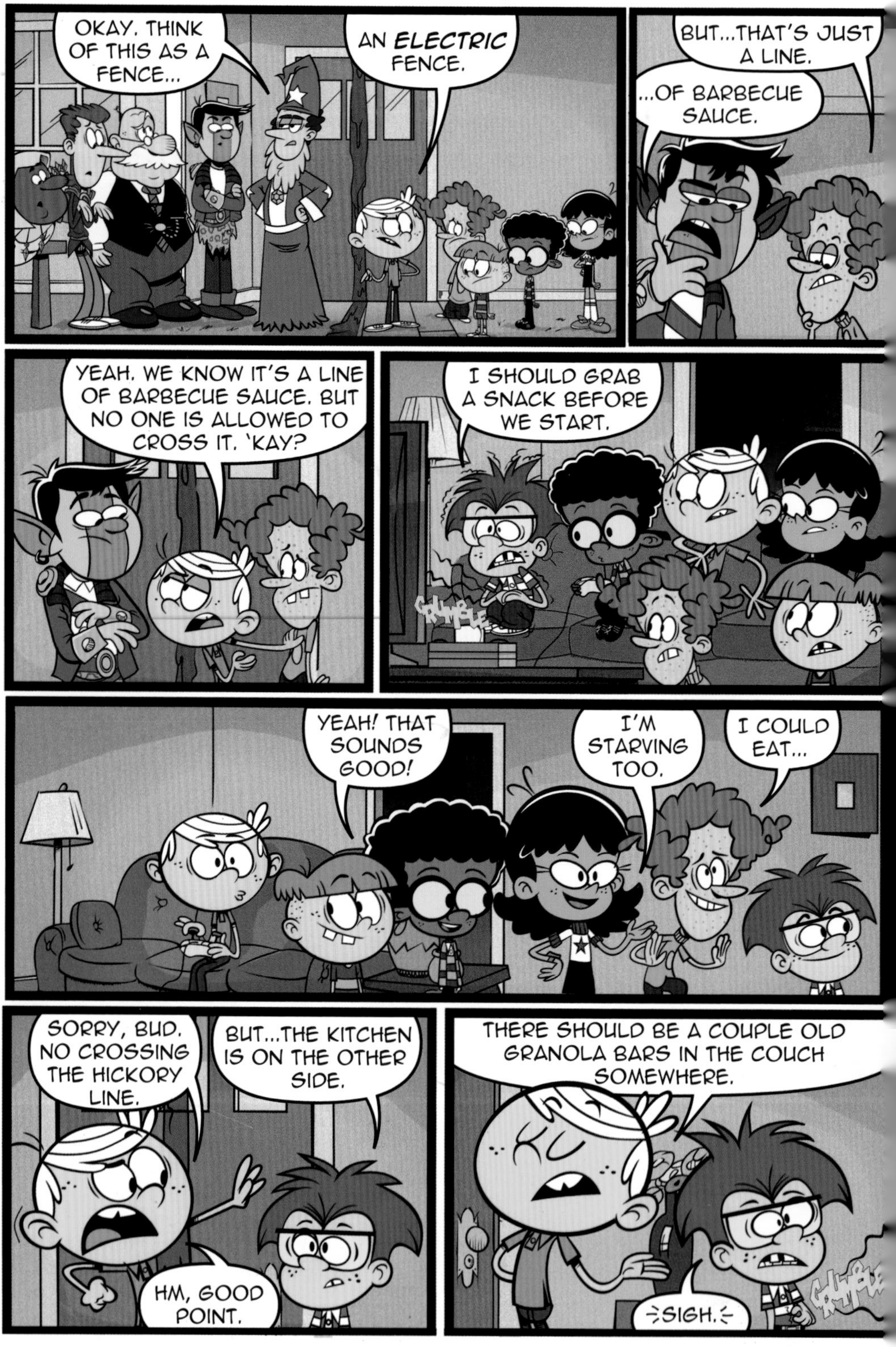
OKAY. THINK OF THIS AS A FENCE...
AN *ELECTRIC* FENCE.
BUT...THAT'S JUST A LINE.
...OF BARBECUE SAUCE.
YEAH. WE KNOW IT'S A LINE OF BARBECUE SAUCE. BUT NO ONE IS ALLOWED TO CROSS IT. 'KAY?
I SHOULD GRAB A SNACK BEFORE WE START.
GRUMBLE
YEAH! THAT SOUNDS GOOD!
I'M STARVING TOO.
I COULD EAT...
SORRY, BUD. NO CROSSING THE HICKORY LINE.
BUT...THE KITCHEN IS ON THE OTHER SIDE.
HM, GOOD POINT.
THERE SHOULD BE A COUPLE OLD GRANOLA BARS IN THE COUCH SOMEWHERE.
SIGH.
GRUMBLE

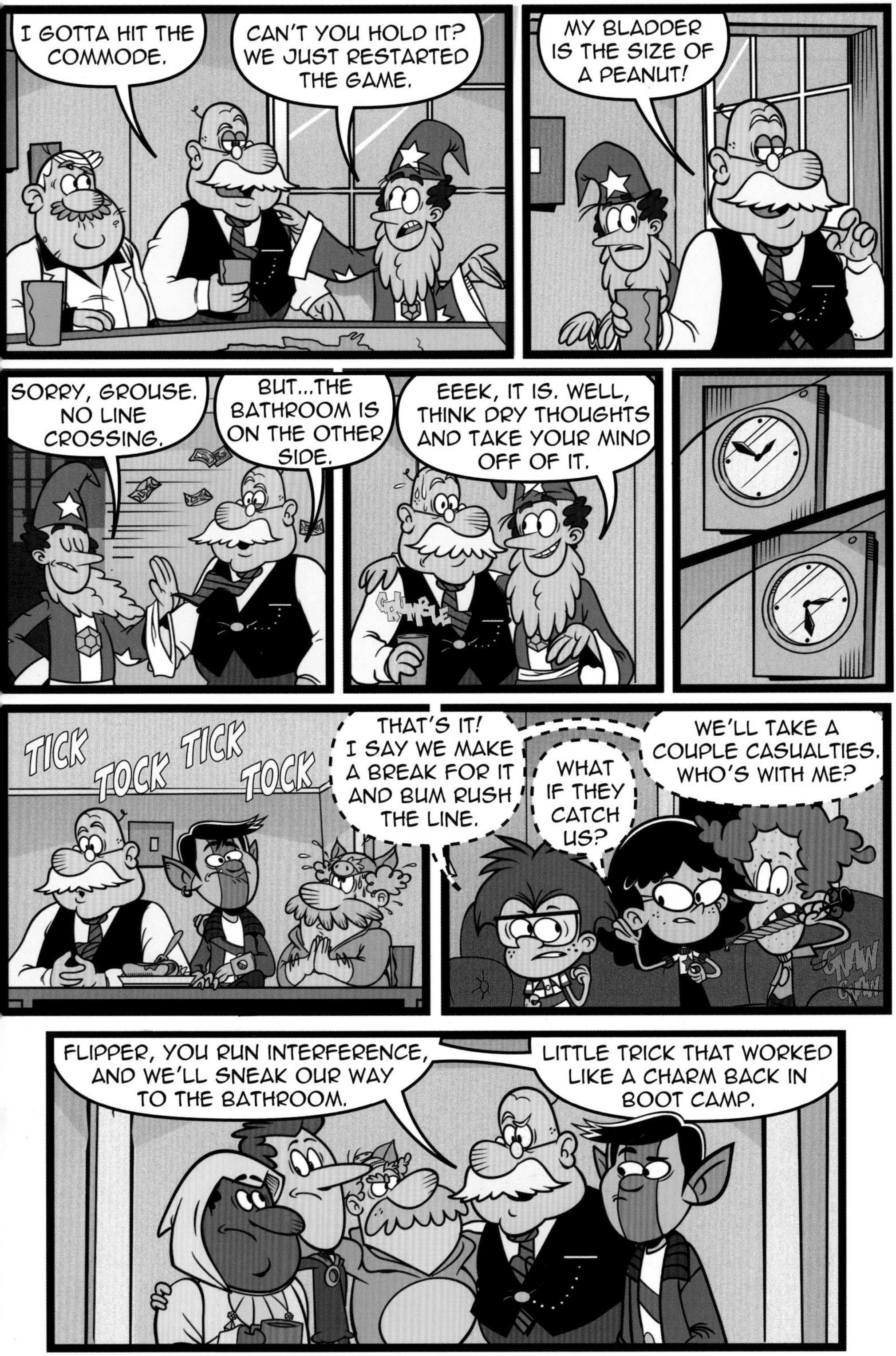
I GOTTA HIT THE COMMODE.
CAN'T YOU HOLD IT? WE JUST RESTARTED THE GAME.
MY BLADDER IS THE SIZE OF A PEANUT!
SORRY, GROUSE. NO LINE CROSSING.
BUT...THE BATHROOM IS ON THE OTHER SIDE.
GRUMBLE
EEEK, IT IS. WELL, THINK DRY THOUGHTS AND TAKE YOUR MIND OFF OF IT.
TICK TOCK TICK TOCK
THAT'S IT! I SAY WE MAKE A BREAK FOR IT AND BUM RUSH THE LINE.
WHAT IF THEY CATCH US?
WE'LL TAKE A COUPLE CASUALTIES. WHO'S WITH ME?
GNAW GNAW
FLIPPER, YOU RUN INTERFERENCE, AND WE'LL SNEAK OUR WAY TO THE BATHROOM.
LITTLE TRICK THAT WORKED LIKE A CHARM BACK IN BOOT CAMP.

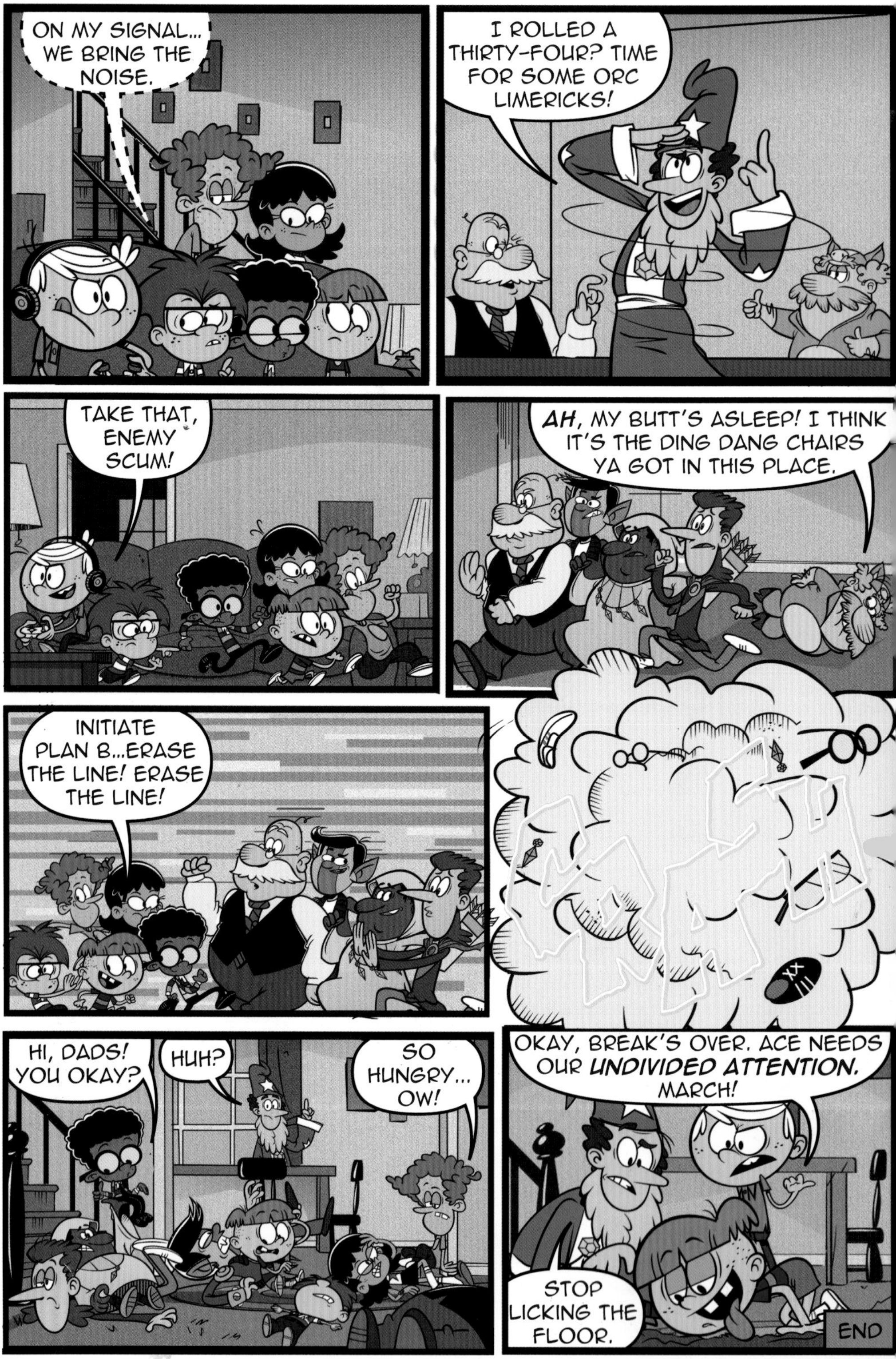
ON MY SIGNAL... WE BRING THE NOISE.
I ROLLED A THIRTY-FOUR? TIME FOR SOME ORC LIMERICKS!
TAKE THAT, ENEMY SCUM!
AH, MY BUTT'S ASLEEP! I THINK IT'S THE DING DANG CHAIRS YA GOT IN THIS PLACE.
INITIATE PLAN B...ERASE THE LINE! ERASE THE LINE!
HI, DADS! YOU OKAY?
HUH?
SO HUNGRY... OW!
OKAY, BREAK'S OVER. ACE NEEDS OUR UNDIVIDED ATTENTION. MARCH!
STOP LICKING THE FLOOR.
END

"NO STRINGS"

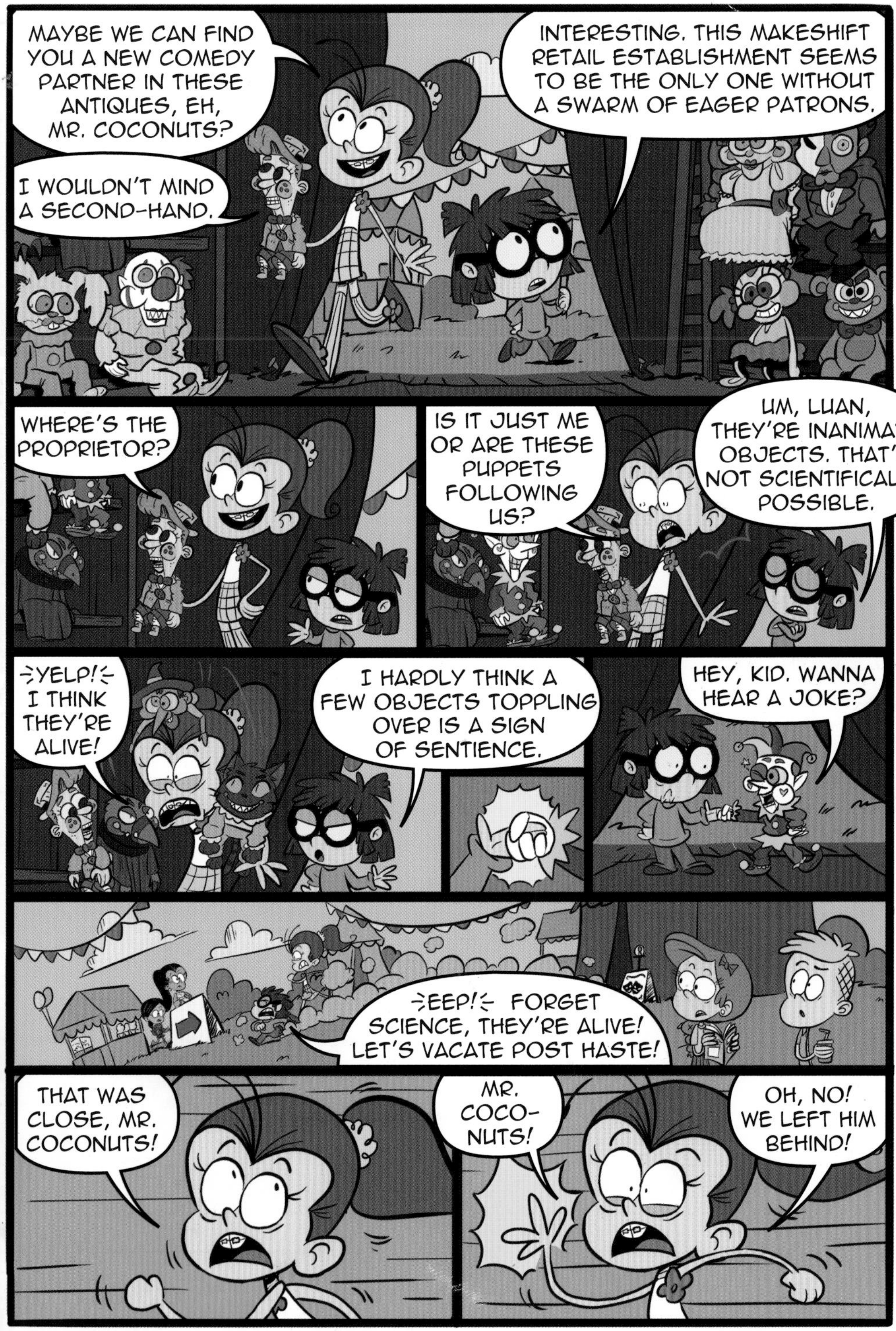
MAYBE WE CAN FIND YOU A NEW COMEDY PARTNER IN THESE ANTIQUES, EH, MR. COCONUTS?
I WOULDN'T MIND A SECOND-HAND.
INTERESTING. THIS MAKESHIFT RETAIL ESTABLISHMENT SEEMS TO BE THE ONLY ONE WITHOUT A SWARM OF EAGER PATRONS.
WHERE'S THE PROPRIETOR?
IS IT JUST ME OR ARE THESE PUPPETS FOLLOWING US?
UM, LUAN, THEY'RE INANIMATE OBJECTS. THAT'S NOT SCIENTIFICALLY POSSIBLE.
YELP! I THINK THEY'RE ALIVE!
I HARDLY THINK A FEW OBJECTS TOPPLING OVER IS A SIGN OF SENTIENCE.
HEY, KID. WANNA HEAR A JOKE?
EEP! FORGET SCIENCE, THEY'RE ALIVE! LET'S VACATE POST HASTE!
THAT WAS CLOSE, MR. COCONUTS!
MR. COCO-NUTS!
OH, NO! WE LEFT HIM BEHIND!

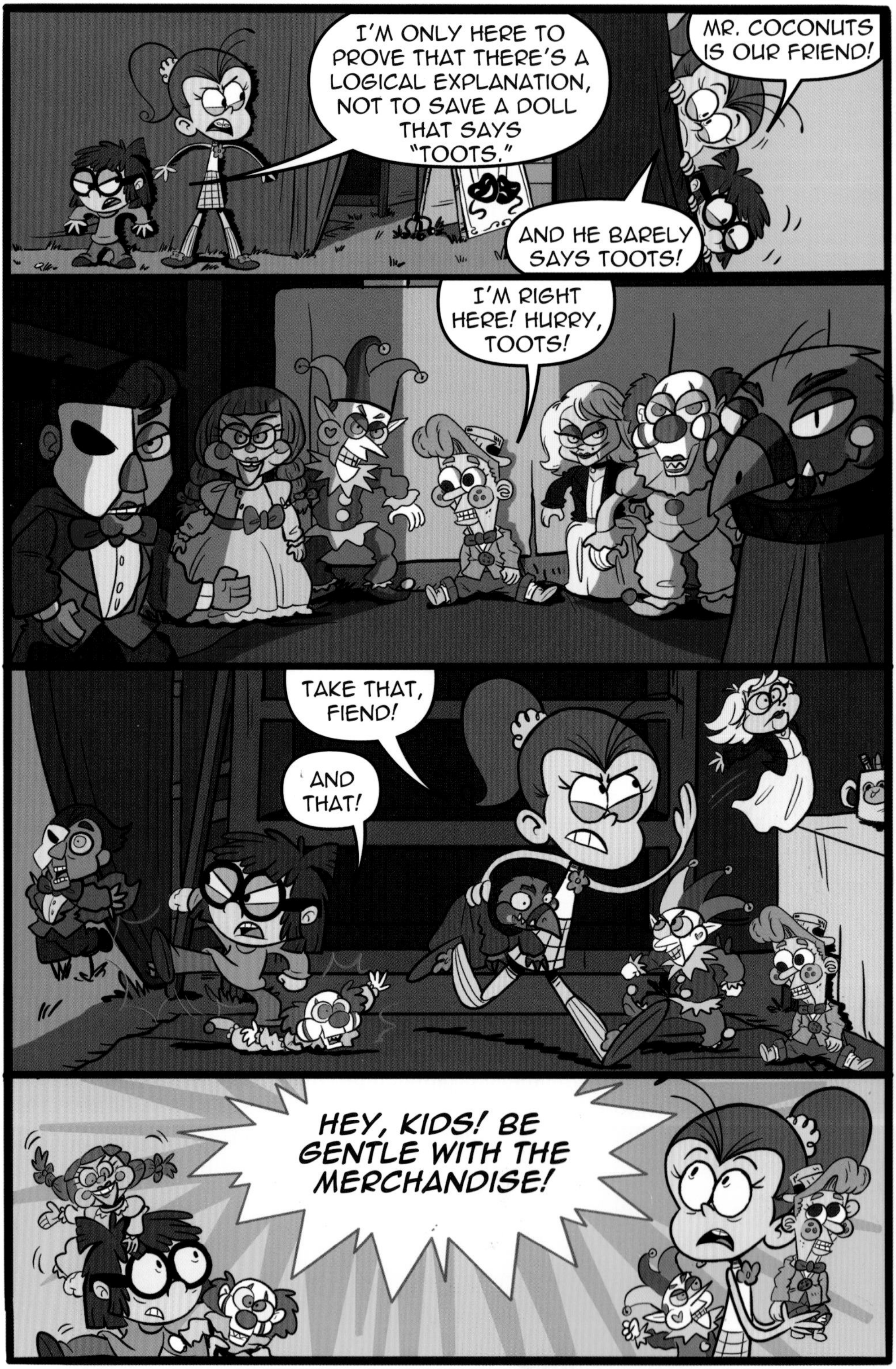
I'M ONLY HERE TO PROVE THAT THERE'S A LOGICAL EXPLANATION, NOT TO SAVE A DOLL THAT SAYS "TOOTS."
MR. COCONUTS IS OUR FRIEND!
AND HE BARELY SAYS TOOTS!
I'M RIGHT HERE! HURRY, TOOTS!
TAKE THAT, FIEND!
AND THAT!
HEY, KIDS! BE GENTLE WITH THE MERCHANDISE!

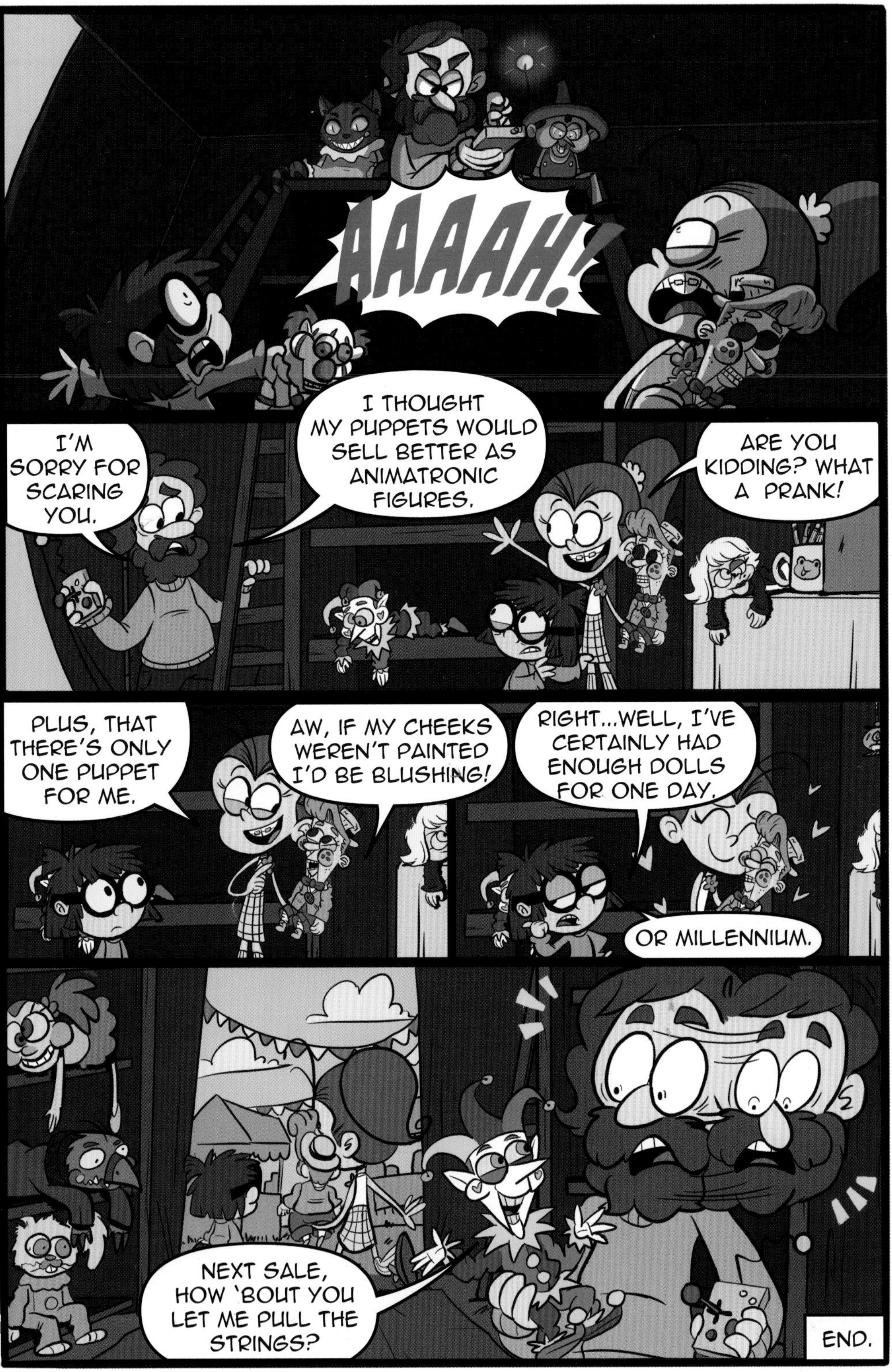

AAAAH!
I'M SORRY FOR SCARING YOU.
I THOUGHT MY PUPPETS WOULD SELL BETTER AS ANIMATRONIC FIGURES.
ARE YOU KIDDING? WHAT A PRANK!
PLUS, THAT THERE'S ONLY ONE PUPPET FOR ME.
AW, IF MY CHEEKS WEREN'T PAINTED I'D BE BLUSHING!
RIGHT...WELL, I'VE CERTAINLY HAD ENOUGH DOLLS FOR ONE DAY.
OR MILLENNIUM.
NEXT SALE, HOW 'BOUT YOU LET ME PULL THE STRINGS?
END.

"SLAM JUNK"

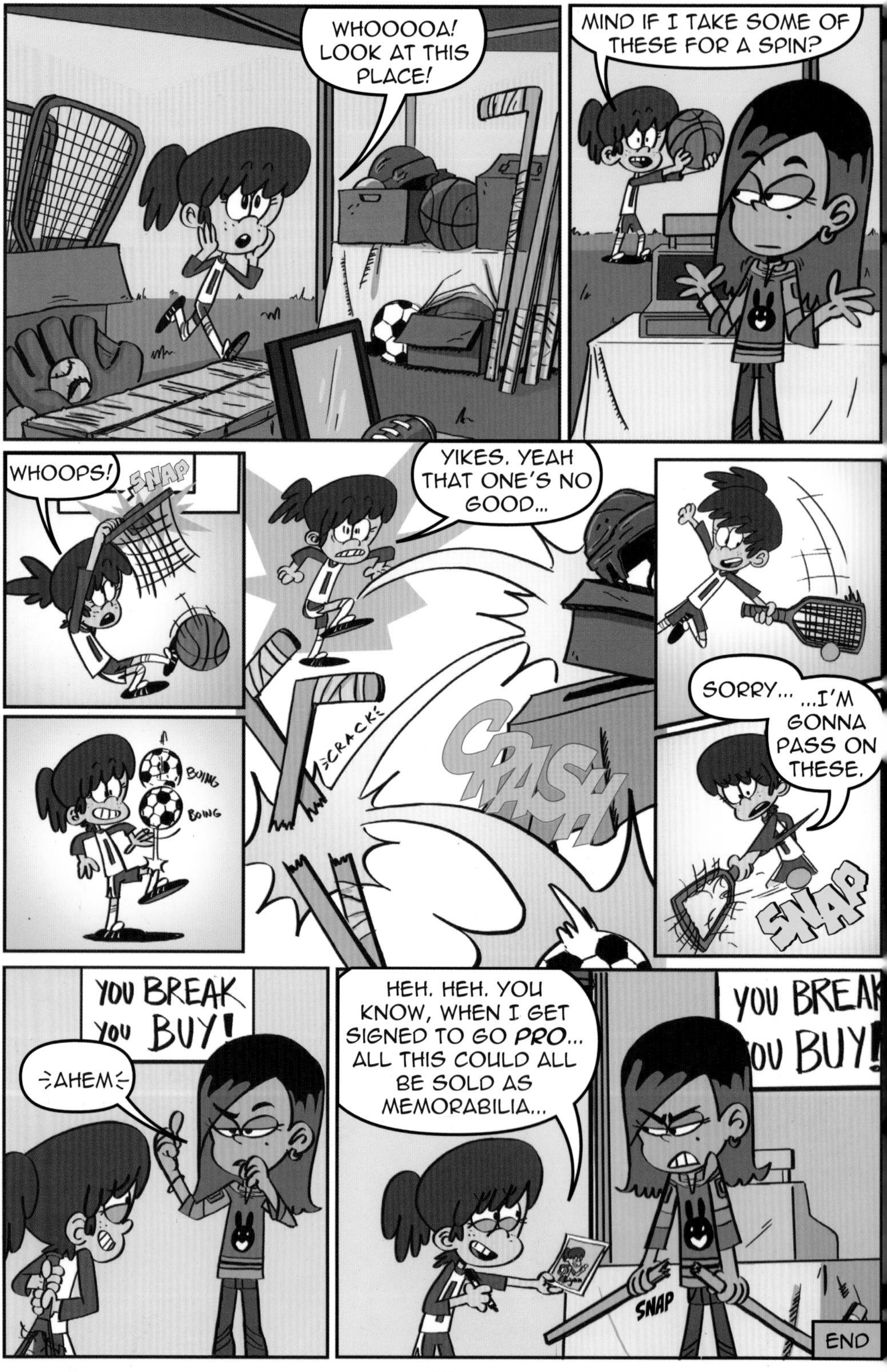
WHOOOOA! LOOK AT THIS PLACE!
MIND IF I TAKE SOME OF THESE FOR A SPIN?
WHOOPS!
SNAP
YIKES. YEAH THAT ONE'S NO GOOD...
BOING
BOING
CRACK
CRASH
SORRY... ...I'M GONNA PASS ON THESE.
SNAP
YOU BREAK YOU BUY!
AHEM
HEH. HEH. YOU KNOW, WHEN I GET SIGNED TO GO *PRO*... ALL THIS COULD ALL BE SOLD AS MEMORABILIA...
YOU BREAK YOU BUY!
SNAP
END

"IT'S MY PARTY"

YAHOO! THE NEXT LEVEL! ISN'T PLAYING MUCH EASIER NOW THAT WE'RE INTERRUPTION-FREE?!

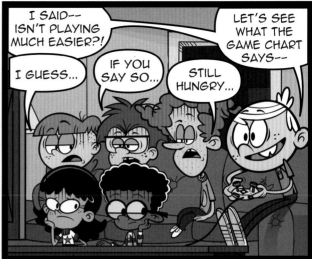

I SAID-- ISN'T PLAYING MUCH EASIER?!

I GUESS...

IF YOU SAY SO...

STILL HUNGRY...

LET'S SEE WHAT THE GAME CHART SAYS--

NOT IMPORTANT! IT'S LIAM'S TURN TO PLAY *SAVVAGE MODE* WITH ME!

SHUCKS, LINC, BUT I'D PREFER TO SIT OUT THIS ROUND.

NO WAY! THIS CONTROLLER HAS YOUR NAME ON IT!

MAN. AND I THOUGHT THE ONLY VILLAIN WOULD BE IN THE VIDEO GAME...

WHEN DID HE EVEN HAVE TIME TO MAKE *THAT*?!

LINE OR NO LINE, WE'VE GOT TO GET OUT OF HERE! MAYBE YOU CAN SEND SOME TYPE OF SIGNAL TO YOUR DADS?

THERE MIGHT BE A WAY. HAND ME ONE OF THOSE GOOSE DOWN PILLOWS.

BUT YOUR ALLERGIES!

TRUST ME.

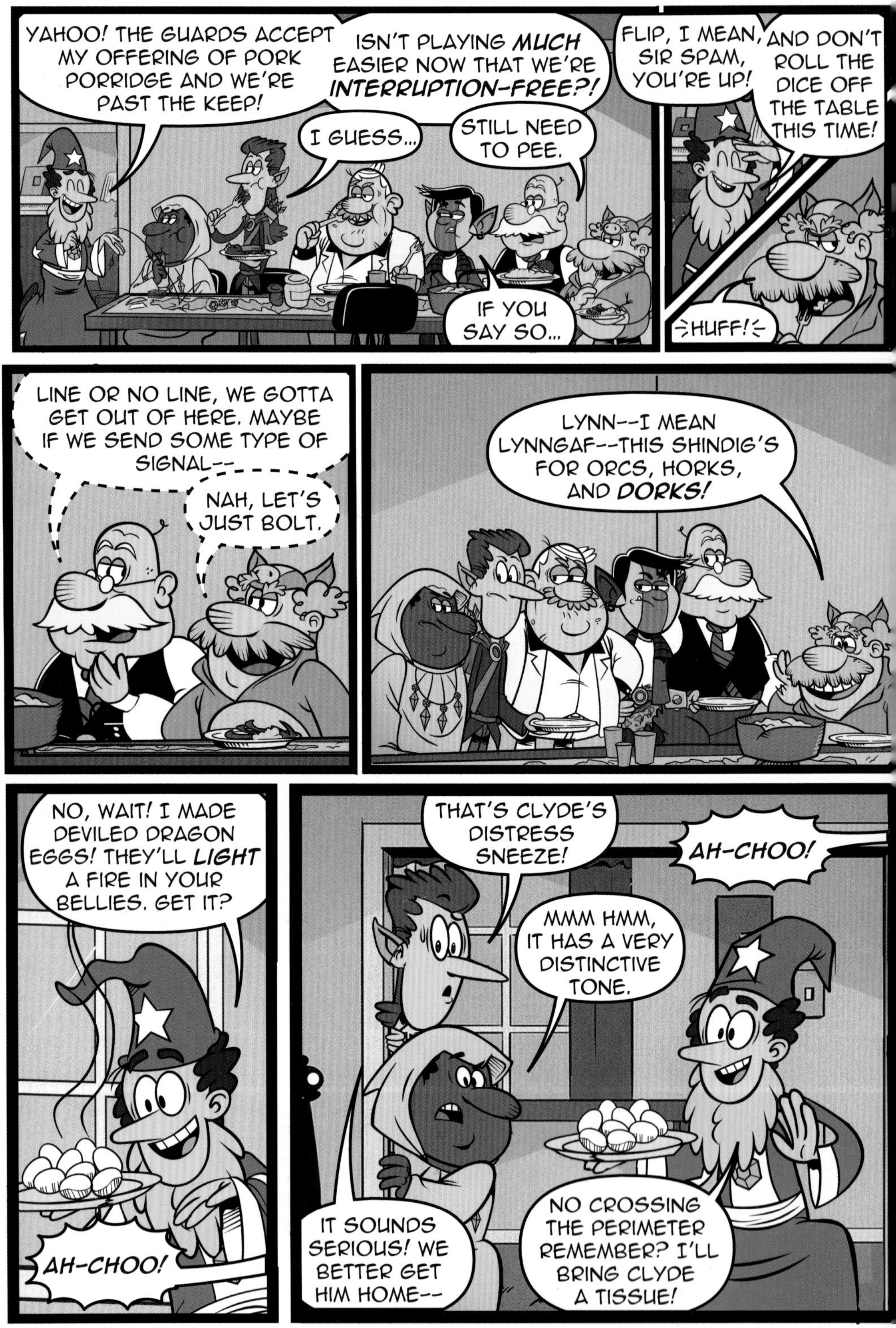
YAHOO! THE GUARDS ACCEPT MY OFFERING OF PORK PORRIDGE AND WE'RE PAST THE KEEP!
ISN'T PLAYING *MUCH* EASIER NOW THAT WE'RE *INTERRUPTION-FREE?!*
I GUESS...
STILL NEED TO PEE.
IF YOU SAY SO...
FLIP, I MEAN, SIR SPAM, YOU'RE UP!
AND DON'T ROLL THE DICE OFF THE TABLE THIS TIME!
HUFF!
LINE OR NO LINE, WE GOTTA GET OUT OF HERE. MAYBE IF WE SEND SOME TYPE OF SIGNAL--
NAH, LET'S JUST BOLT.
LYNN--I MEAN LYNNGAF--THIS SHINDIG'S FOR ORCS, HORKS, AND *DORKS!*
NO, WAIT! I MADE DEVILED DRAGON EGGS! THEY'LL *LIGHT* A FIRE IN YOUR BELLIES. GET IT?
AH-CHOO!
THAT'S CLYDE'S DISTRESS SNEEZE!
AH-CHOO!
MMM HMM, IT HAS A VERY DISTINCTIVE TONE.
IT SOUNDS SERIOUS! WE BETTER GET HIM HOME--
NO CROSSING THE PERIMETER REMEMBER? I'LL BRING CLYDE A TISSUE!

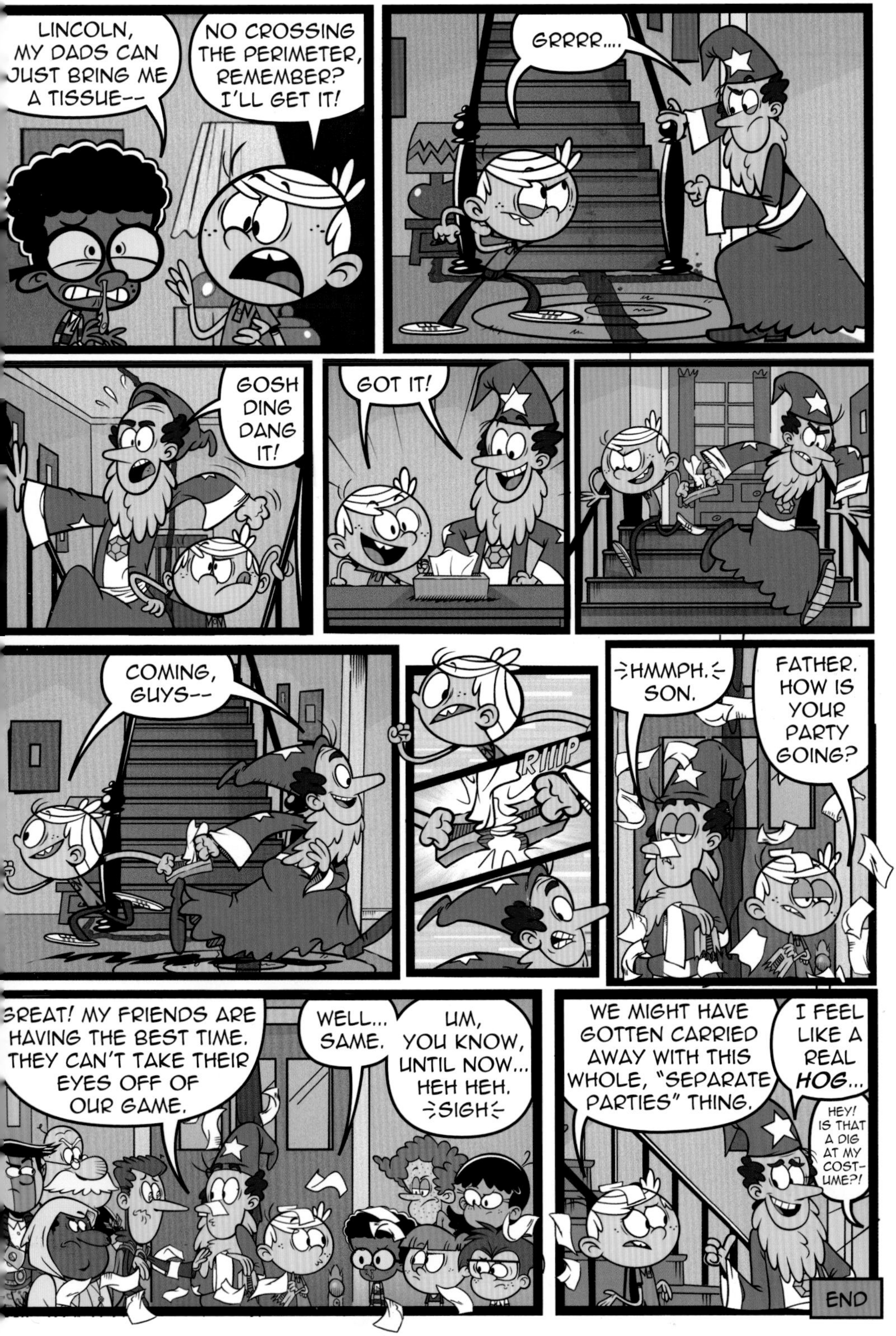

LINCOLN, MY DADS CAN JUST BRING ME A TISSUE--
NO CROSSING THE PERIMETER, REMEMBER? I'LL GET IT!
GRRRR....
GOSH DING DANG IT!
GOT IT!
COMING, GUYS--
RIIIP
HMMPH. SON.
FATHER. HOW IS YOUR PARTY GOING?
GREAT! MY FRIENDS ARE HAVING THE BEST TIME. THEY CAN'T TAKE THEIR EYES OFF OF OUR GAME.
WELL... SAME.
UM, YOU KNOW, UNTIL NOW... HEH HEH. SIGH
WE MIGHT HAVE GOTTEN CARRIED AWAY WITH THIS WHOLE, "SEPARATE PARTIES" THING.
I FEEL LIKE A REAL HOG...
HEY! IS THAT A DIG AT MY COSTUME?!
END

"EYE ON THE BALL"

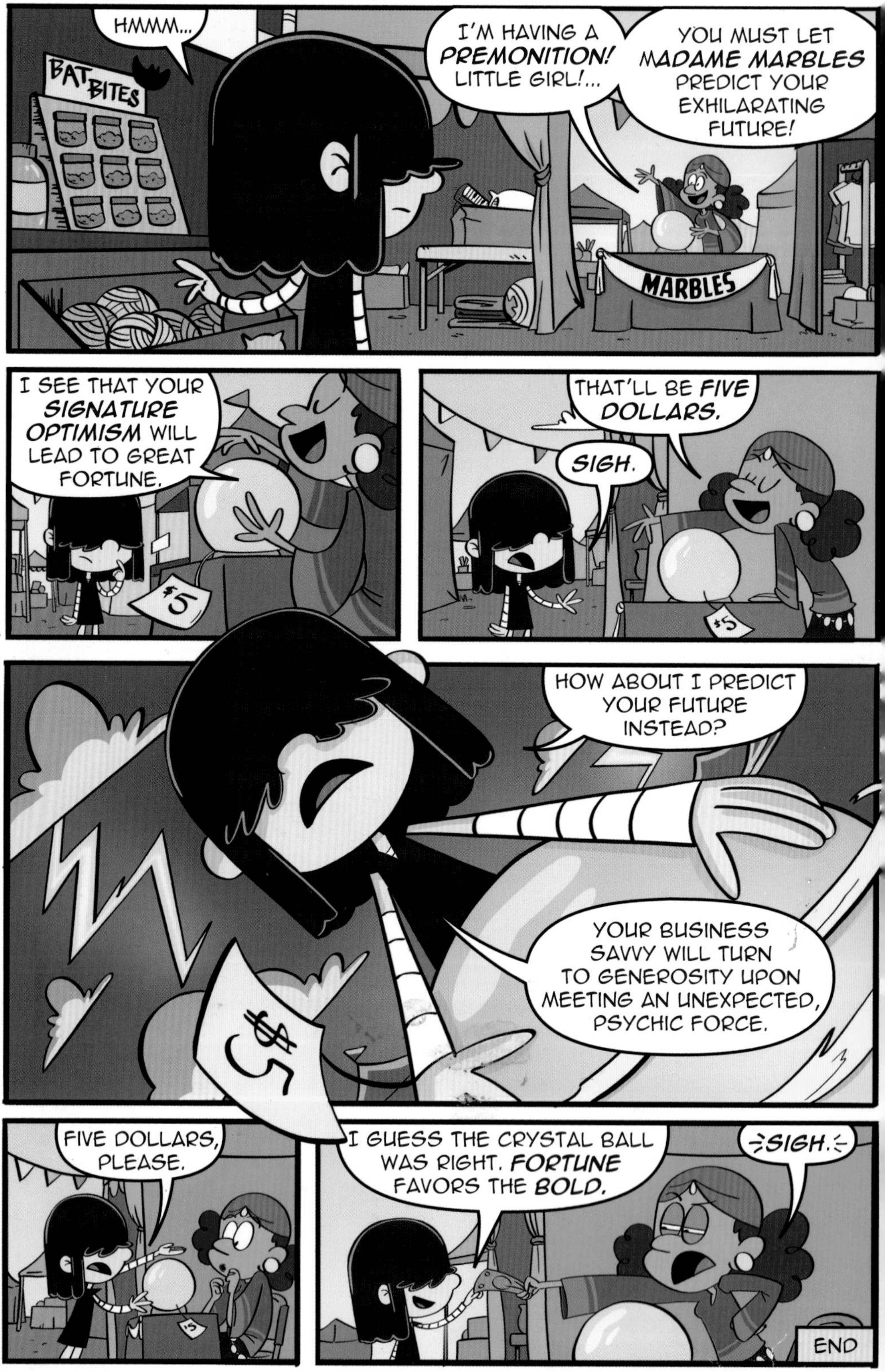

HMMM...
BAT BITES
I'M HAVING A PREMONITION! LITTLE GIRL!...
YOU MUST LET MADAME MARBLES PREDICT YOUR EXHILARATING FUTURE!
MARBLES
I SEE THAT YOUR SIGNATURE OPTIMISM WILL LEAD TO GREAT FORTUNE.
$5
THAT'LL BE FIVE DOLLARS.
SIGH.
$5
HOW ABOUT I PREDICT YOUR FUTURE INSTEAD?
YOUR BUSINESS SAVVY WILL TURN TO GENEROSITY UPON MEETING AN UNEXPECTED, PSYCHIC FORCE.
$5
FIVE DOLLARS, PLEASE.
$5
I GUESS THE CRYSTAL BALL WAS RIGHT. FORTUNE FAVORS THE BOLD.
SIGH.
END

"THE PERFECT GIFT"

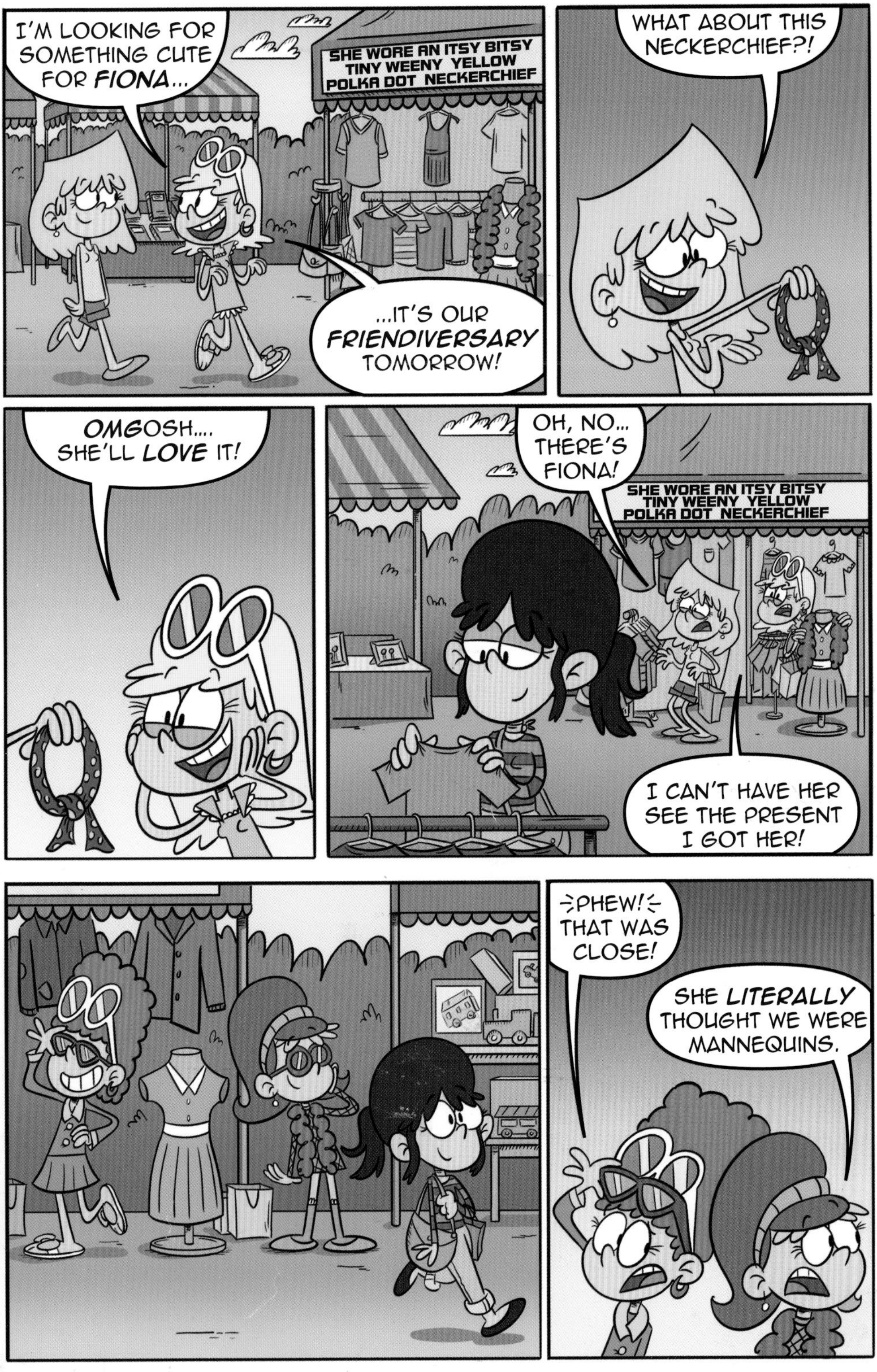
I'M LOOKING FOR SOMETHING CUTE FOR FIONA...
SHE WORE AN ITSY BITSY TINY WEENY YELLOW POLKA DOT NECKERCHIEF
...IT'S OUR FRIENDIVERSARY TOMORROW!
WHAT ABOUT THIS NECKERCHIEF?!
OMGOSH.... SHE'LL LOVE IT!
OH, NO... THERE'S FIONA!
SHE WORE AN ITSY BITSY TINY WEENY YELLOW POLKA DOT NECKERCHIEF
I CAN'T HAVE HER SEE THE PRESENT I GOT HER!
PHEW! THAT WAS CLOSE!
SHE LITERALLY THOUGHT WE WERE MANNEQUINS.

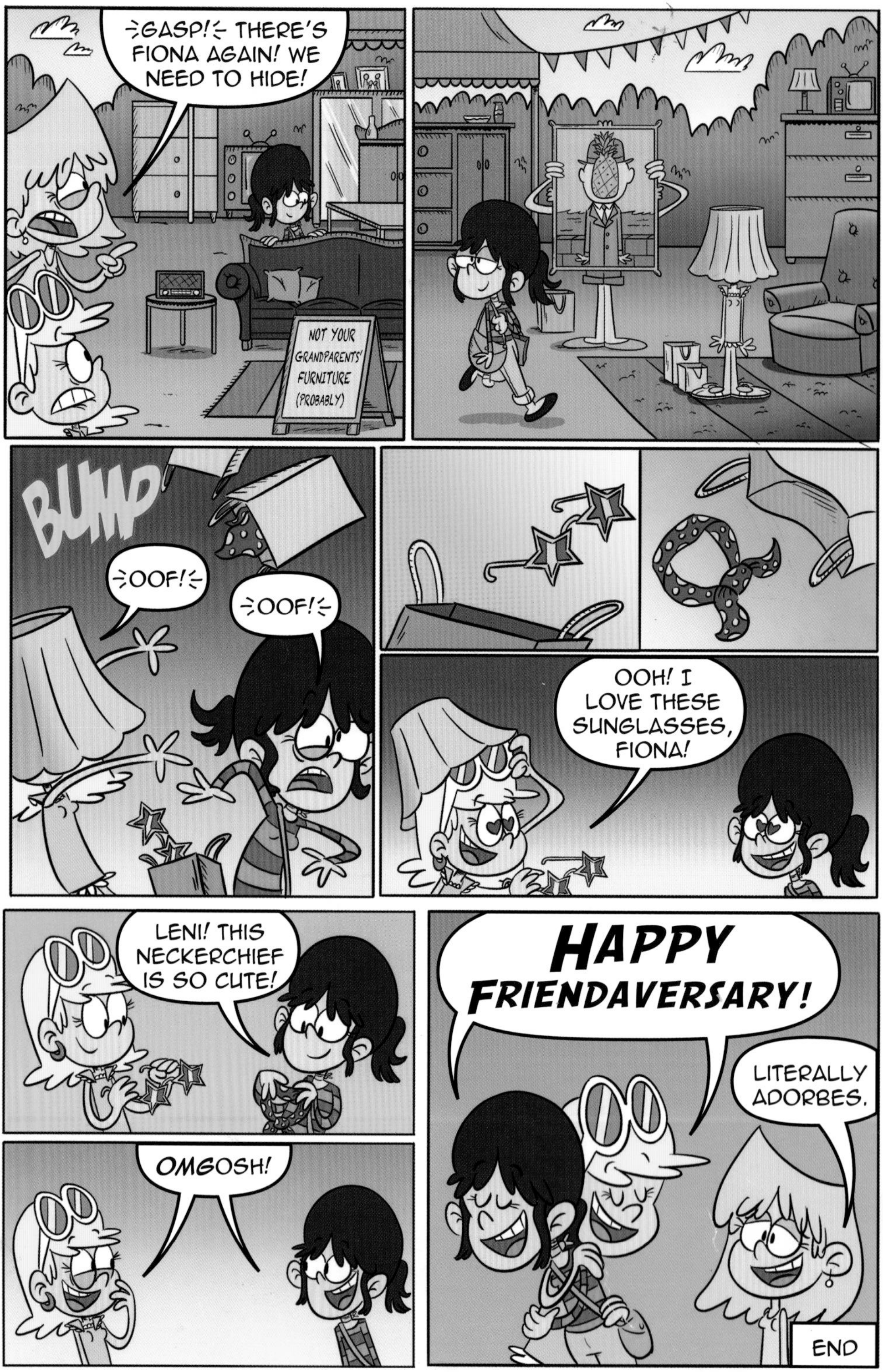
GASP! THERE'S FIONA AGAIN! WE NEED TO HIDE!
NOT YOUR GRANDPARENTS' FURNITURE (PROBABLY)
BUMP
OOF!
OOF!
OOH! I LOVE THESE SUNGLASSES, FIONA!
LENI! THIS NECKERCHIEF IS SO CUTE!
OMGOSH!
HAPPY FRIENDAVERSARY!
LITERALLY ADORBES.
END

"FLEA RIDDLE"

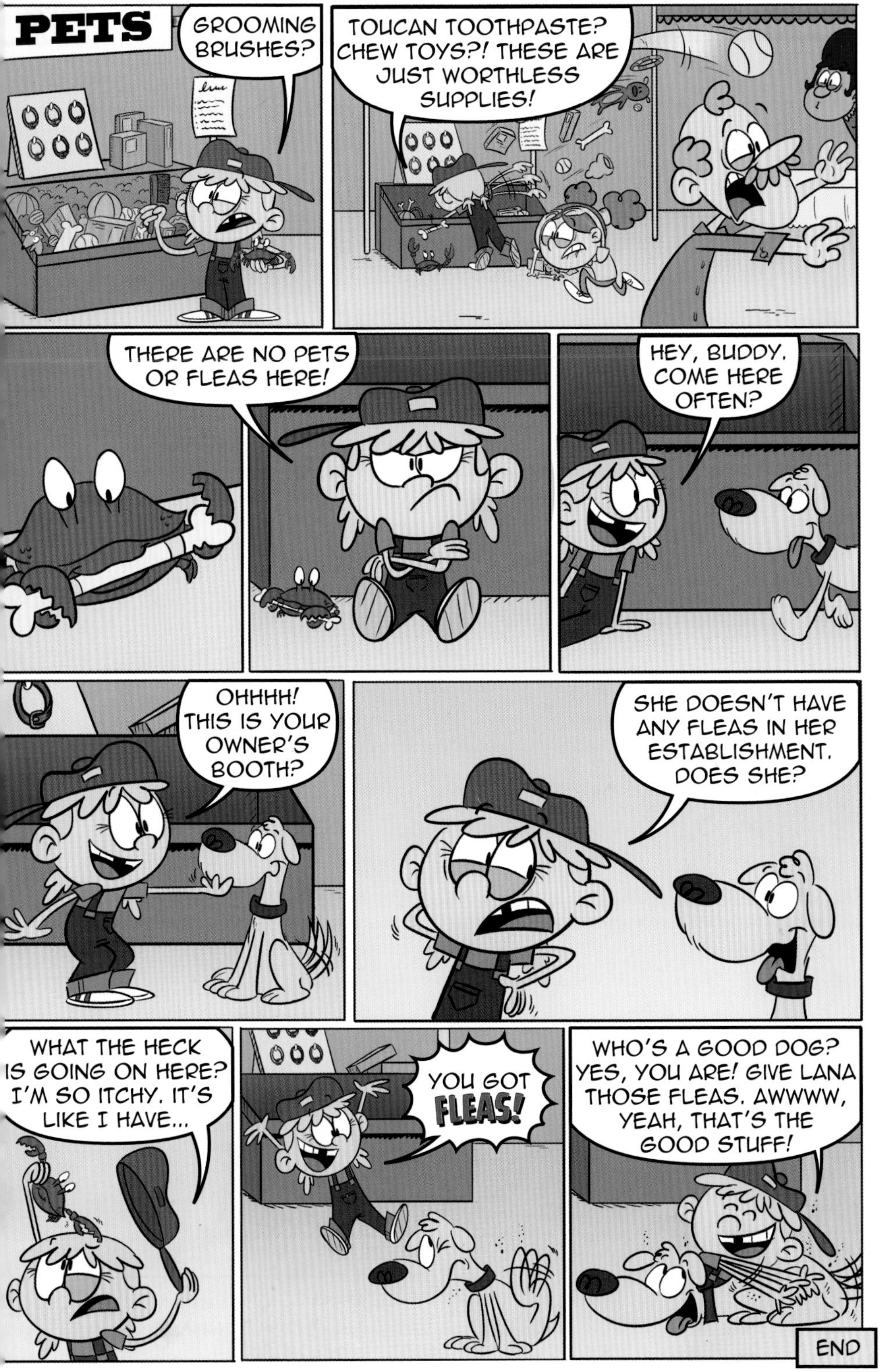
PETS
GROOMING BRUSHES?
TOUCAN TOOTHPASTE? CHEW TOYS?! THESE ARE JUST WORTHLESS SUPPLIES!
THERE ARE NO PETS OR FLEAS HERE!
HEY, BUDDY. COME HERE OFTEN?
OHHHH! THIS IS YOUR OWNER'S BOOTH?
SHE DOESN'T HAVE ANY FLEAS IN HER ESTABLISHMENT. DOES SHE?
WHAT THE HECK IS GOING ON HERE? I'M SO ITCHY. IT'S LIKE I HAVE...
YOU GOT FLEAS!
WHO'S A GOOD DOG? YES, YOU ARE! GIVE LANA THOSE FLEAS. AWWWW, YEAH, THAT'S THE GOOD STUFF!
END

"PARTY MIXER"

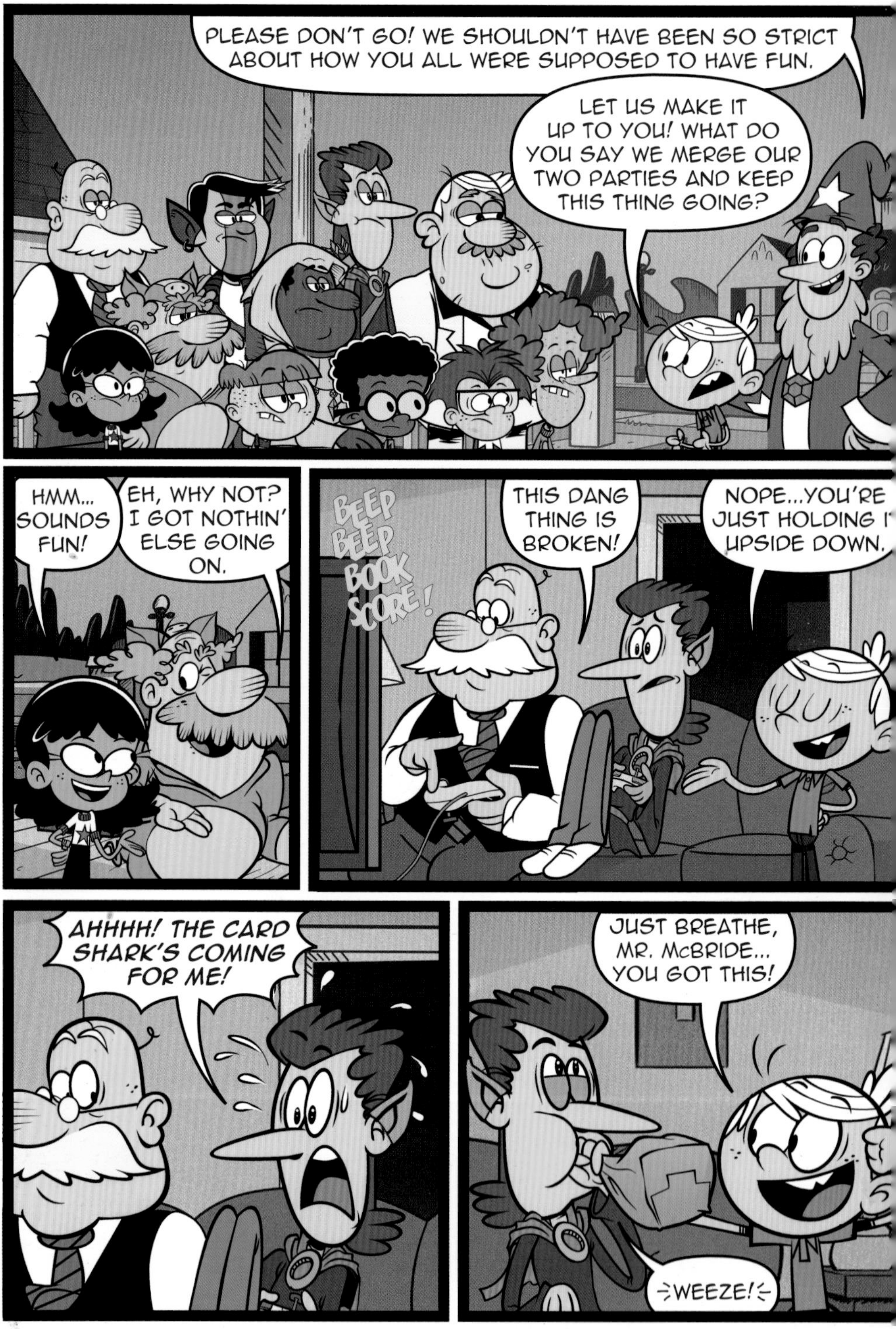
PLEASE DON'T GO! WE SHOULDN'T HAVE BEEN SO STRICT ABOUT HOW YOU ALL WERE SUPPOSED TO HAVE FUN.
LET US MAKE IT UP TO YOU! WHAT DO YOU SAY WE MERGE OUR TWO PARTIES AND KEEP THIS THING GOING?
HMM... SOUNDS FUN!
EH, WHY NOT? I GOT NOTHIN' ELSE GOING ON.
BEEP BEEP BOOK SCORE!
THIS DANG THING IS BROKEN!
NOPE...YOU'RE JUST HOLDING I UPSIDE DOWN.
AHHHH! THE CARD SHARK'S COMING FOR ME!
JUST BREATHE, MR. McBRIDE... YOU GOT THIS!
WEEZE!

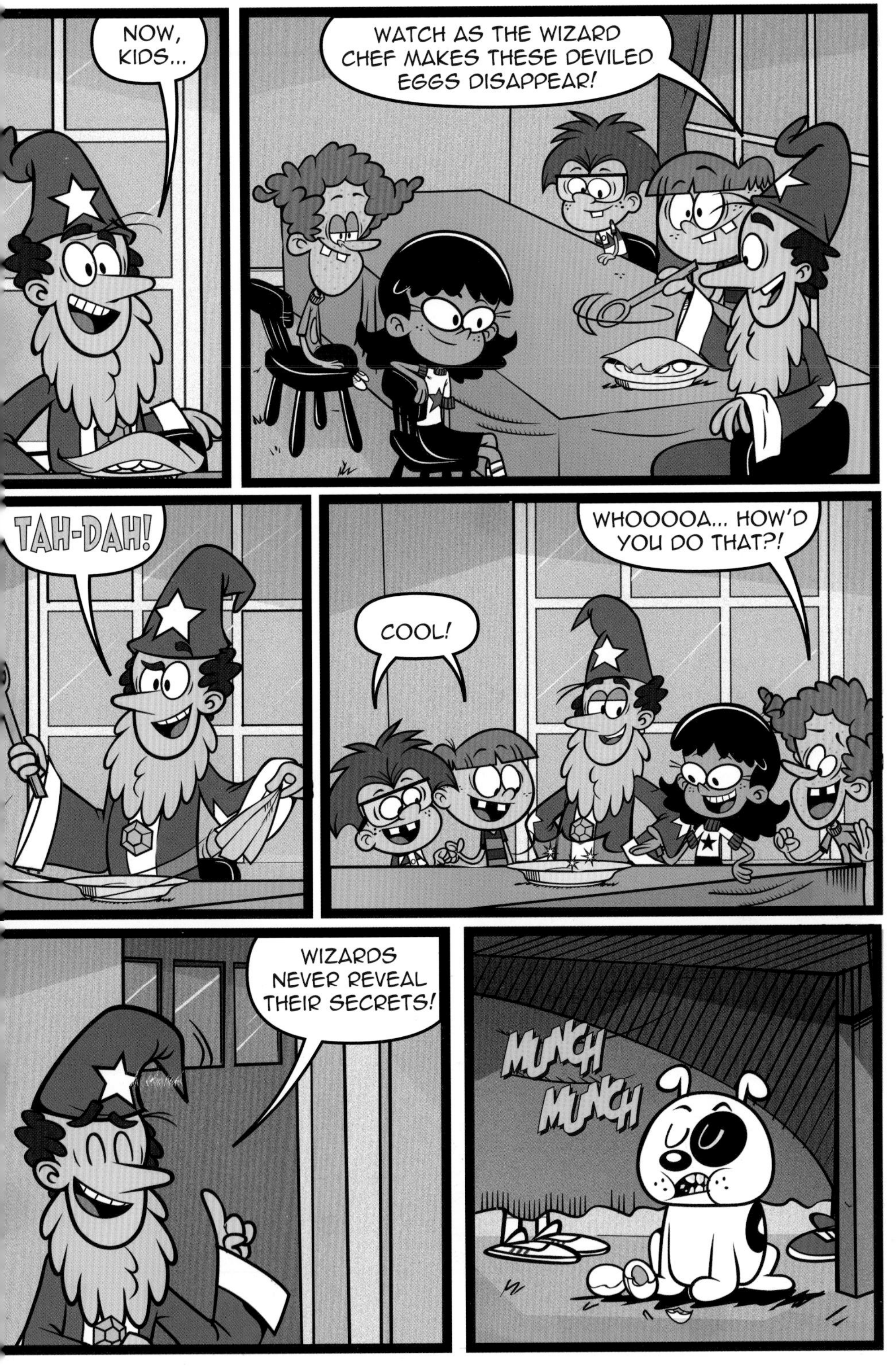
NOW, KIDS...
WATCH AS THE WIZARD CHEF MAKES THESE DEVILED EGGS DISAPPEAR!
TAH-DAH!
WHOOOOA... HOW'D YOU DO THAT?!
COOL!
WIZARDS NEVER REVEAL THEIR SECRETS!
MUNCH
MUNCH

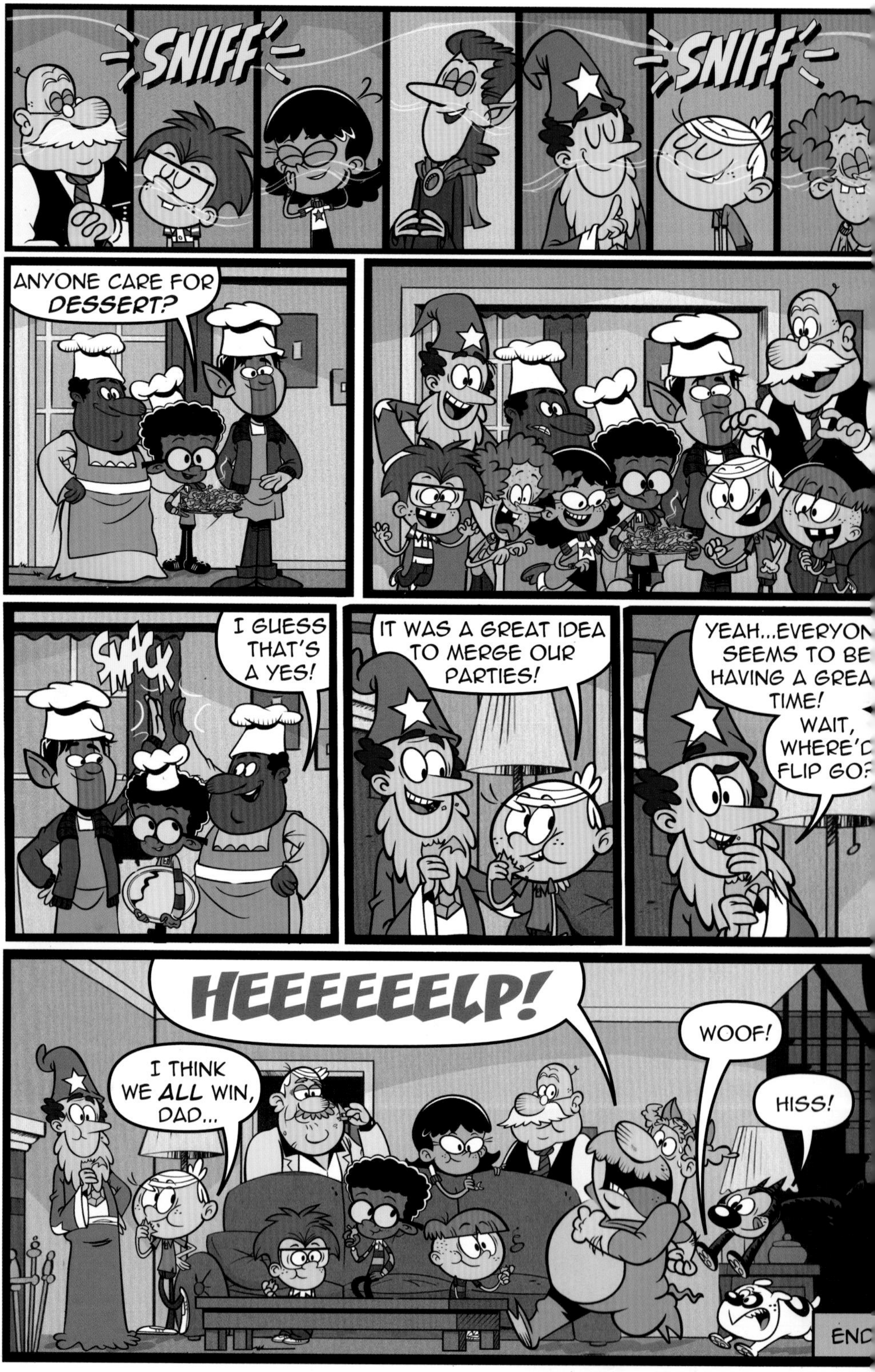
SNIFF
SNIFF
ANYONE CARE FOR DESSERT?
SMACK
I GUESS THAT'S A YES!
IT WAS A GREAT IDEA TO MERGE OUR PARTIES!
YEAH...EVERYON
SEEMS TO BE
HAVING A GREA
TIME!
WAIT, WHERE'D FLIP GO?
HEEEEEELP!
I THINK WE ALL WIN, DAD...
WOOF!
HISS!
END

"THE LONG ROAD HOME"

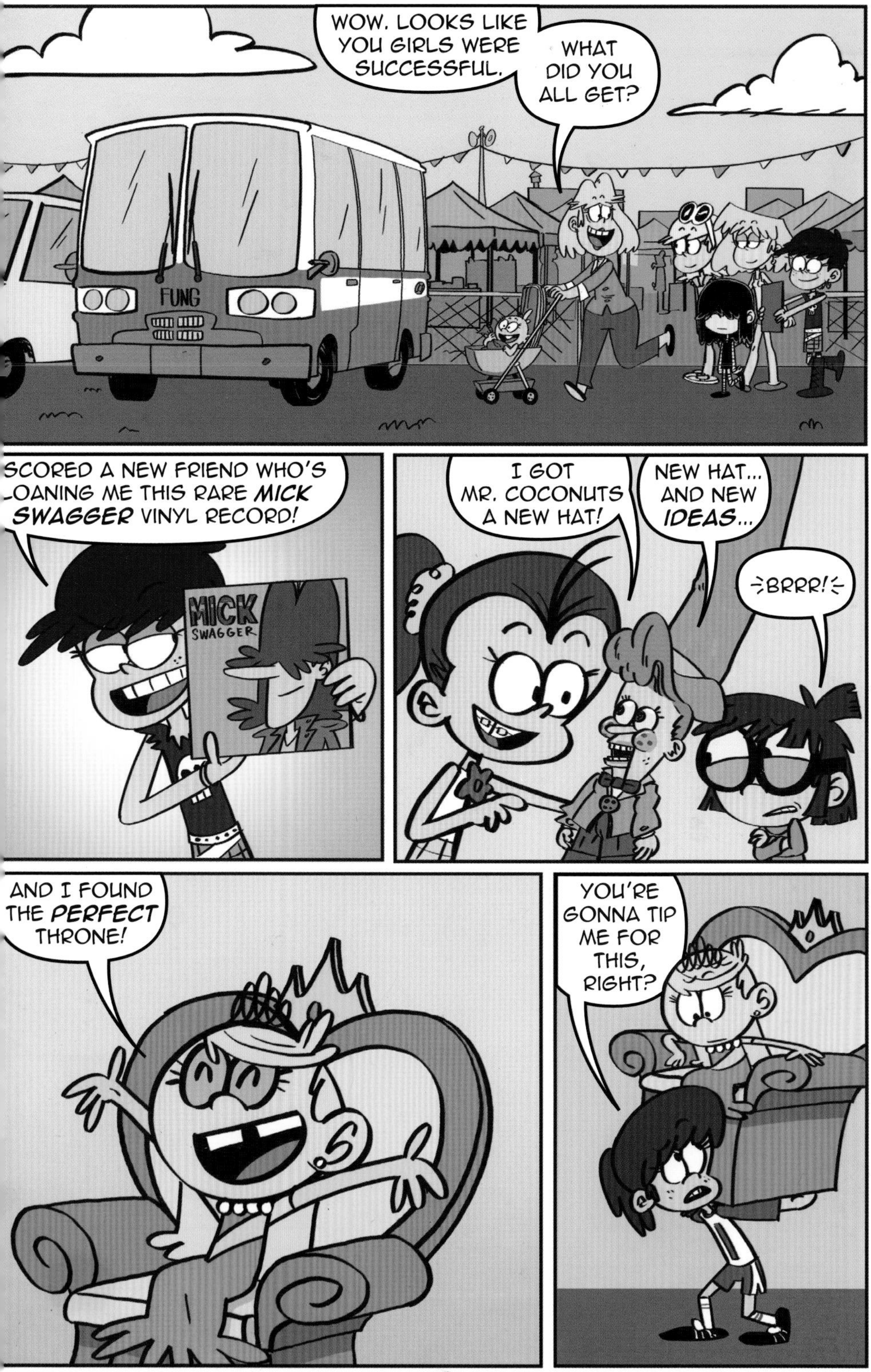
WOW. LOOKS LIKE YOU GIRLS WERE SUCCESSFUL.
WHAT DID YOU ALL GET?
FUNG
SCORED A NEW FRIEND WHO'S LOANING ME THIS RARE *MICK SWAGGER* VINYL RECORD!
MICK SWAGGER
I GOT MR. COCONUTS A NEW HAT!
NEW HAT... AND NEW *IDEAS*...
BRRR!
AND I FOUND THE *PERFECT* THRONE!
YOU'RE GONNA TIP ME FOR THIS, RIGHT?

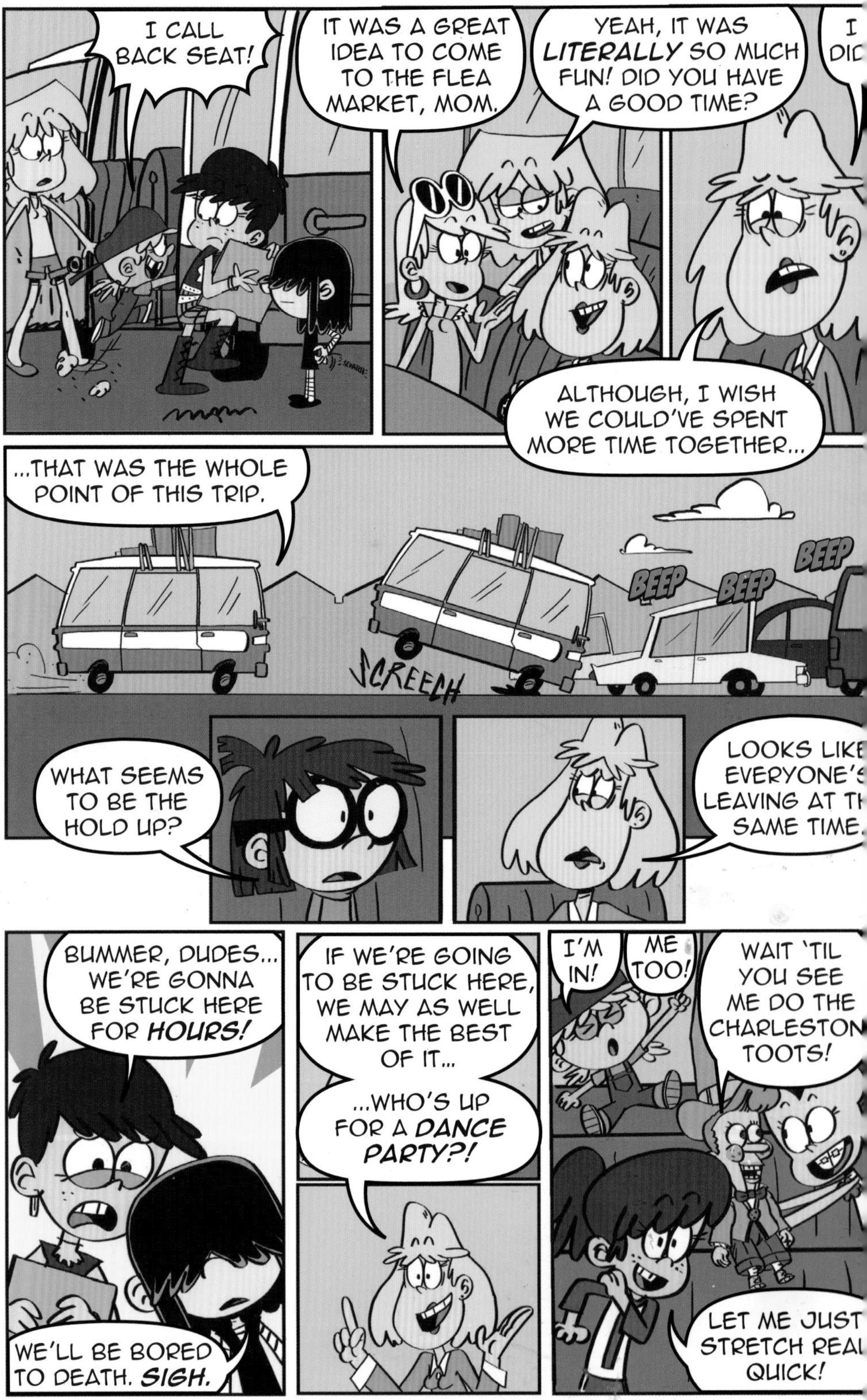
I CALL BACK SEAT!
IT WAS A GREAT IDEA TO COME TO THE FLEA MARKET, MOM.
YEAH, IT WAS LITERALLY SO MUCH FUN! DID YOU HAVE A GOOD TIME?
ALTHOUGH, I WISH WE COULD'VE SPENT MORE TIME TOGETHER...
...THAT WAS THE WHOLE POINT OF THIS TRIP.
SCREECH
BEEP
BEEP
BEEP
WHAT SEEMS TO BE THE HOLD UP?
BUMMER, DUDES... WE'RE GONNA BE STUCK HERE FOR HOURS!
WE'LL BE BORED TO DEATH. SIGH.
IF WE'RE GOING TO BE STUCK HERE, WE MAY AS WELL MAKE THE BEST OF IT...
...WHO'S UP FOR A DANCE PARTY?!
I'M IN!
ME TOO!
LET ME JUST

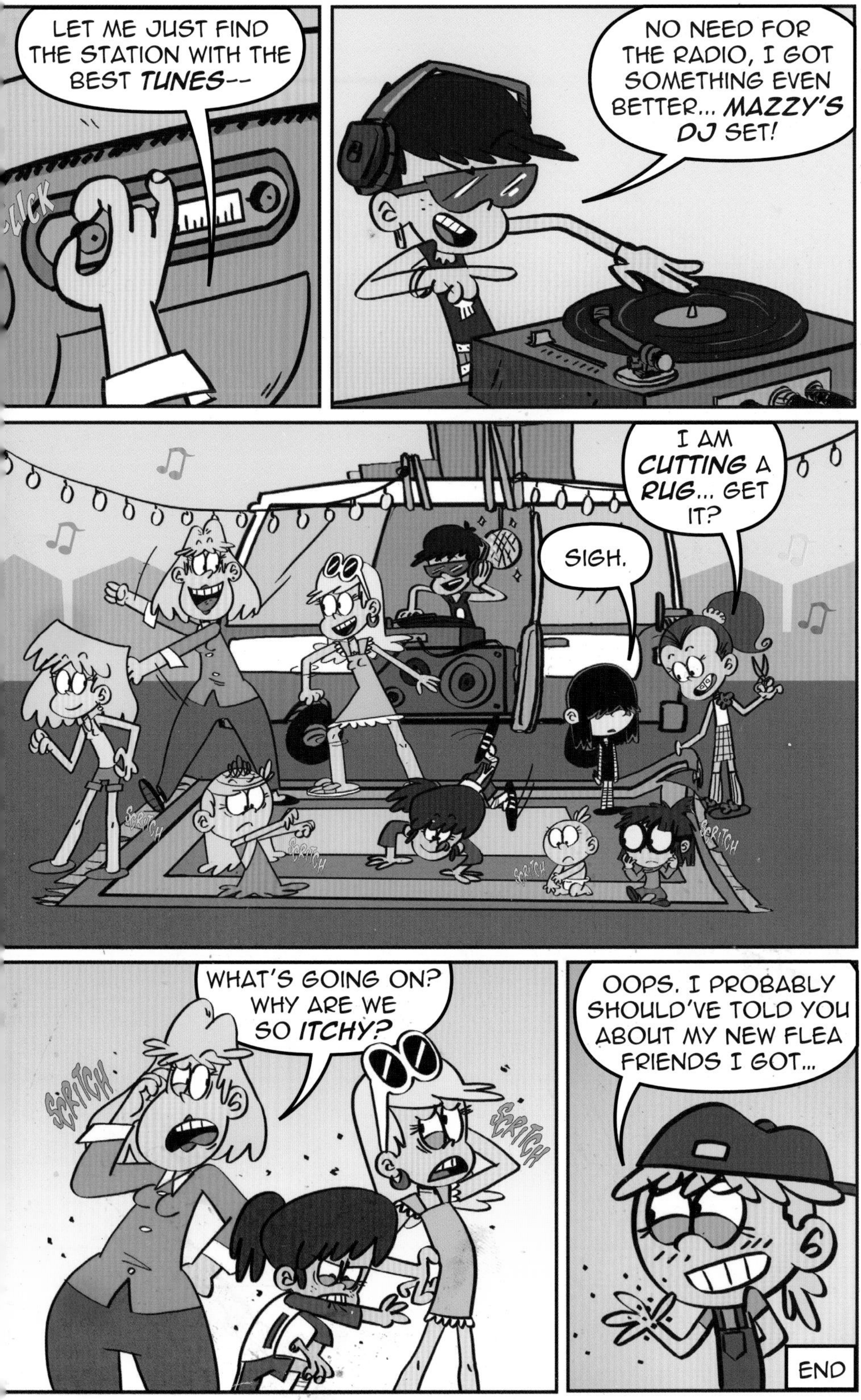
LET ME JUST FIND THE STATION WITH THE BEST TUNES--
CLICK
NO NEED FOR THE RADIO, I GOT SOMETHING EVEN BETTER... MAZZY'S DJ SET!
I AM CUTTING A RUG... GET IT?
SIGH.
SCRITCH
SCRITCH
SCRITCH
SCRITCH
WHAT'S GOING ON? WHY ARE WE SO ITCHY?
SCRITCH
SCRITCH
OOPS. I PROBABLY SHOULD'VE TOLD YOU ABOUT MY NEW FLEA FRIENDS I GOT...
END

COMING SOON

NICKELODEON'S EMMY-WINNING ANIMATED SHOW
nickelodeon
THE LOUD HOUSE
THE MANY FACES OF LINCOLN LOUD

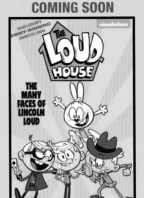

THE LOUD HOUSE
#10
"The Many Faces of
Lincoln Loud"

nickelodeon
3 GRAPHIC NOVELS IN 1
THE LOUD HOUSE
INCLUDES
"THERE WILL BE CHAOS"
"THERE WILL BE MORE CHAOS"
"LIVE LIFE LOUD!"
PAPERCUTZ

THE LOUD HOUSE
3 IN 1
#1

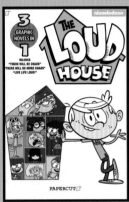

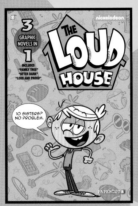

nickelodeon
3 GRAPHIC NOVELS IN 1
THE LOUD HOUSE
INCLUDES
"FAMILY TREE"
"AFTER DARK"
"LOUD AND PROUD"
10 SISTERS? NO PROBLEM.
PAPERCUTZ

THE LOUD HOUSE
3 IN 1
#2

nickelodeon
3 GRAPHIC NOVELS IN 1
THE LOUD HOUSE
INCLUDES
"THE STRUGGLE IS REAL"
"LIVIN' LA CASA LOUD!"
"ULTIMATE HANGOUT"
PAPERCUTZ

THE LOUD HOUSE
3 IN 1
#3

BOXED SET OF 3 GRAPHIC NOVELS
THE LOUD HOUSE
PAPERCUTZ

THE LOUD HOUSE
BOXED SET

OUD HOUSE graphic novels are available for $7.99 each in paperback, $12.99 each in hardcover. LOUD HOUSE 3 IN
 is available for $14.99 each in hardcover only. THE LOUD HOUSE BOXED SET is available for $23.99. Available from
oksellers everywhere. You can also order online from Papercutz.com, or call 1-800-886-1223, Monday through Friday, 9-5
T. MC, Visa, and AmEx accepted. To order by mail, please add $5.00 for postage and handling for the first book ordered,
$1.00 for each additional book and make check payable to NBM Publishing.
Send to: Papercutz, 160 Broadway, Suite 700, East Wing, New York, NY 10038.

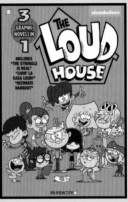

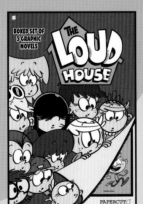

WATCH OUT FOR PAPERCUTZ

Welcome to the nutty, never-naughty, ninth THE LOUD HOUSE graphic novel "Ultimate Hangout," from Papercu those merry mallrats dedicated to publishing great graphic novels for all ages. I'm Jim Salicrup, Editor-in-Chief ar the Ultimate Hanger-Outer at the palatial Papercutz offices, where I tend to binge-watch The Loud House and Th Casagrandes on Nickelodeon, when no one's looking. I'm really excited to announce that in addition to producing many THE LOUD HOUSE graphic novels as possible (to meet the insatiable demand), as well as assembling all o other incredible graphic novels, we got some exciting Papercutz publishing news—so exciting, it was even in the Ne York Times! So exciting, I'm going to tell you all about it right now...

Papercutz has managed to get the North American rights to publish perhaps the most successful comics series in the world—ASTERIX! Now some of you may not have heard of this Asterix fella, so let's take a quick journey in the Papercutz time machine...

We're back in the year 50 BC in the ancient country of Gaul, located where France, Belgium, and the Southern Netherlands are today. All of Gaul has been conquered by the Romans... well, not all of it. One tiny village, inhabited by indomitable Gauls, resists the invaders again and again. That doesn't make it easy for the garrisons of Roman soldiers surrounding the village in fortified camps. So, how's it possible that a small village can hold its own against the mighty Roman Empire? The answer is this guy...

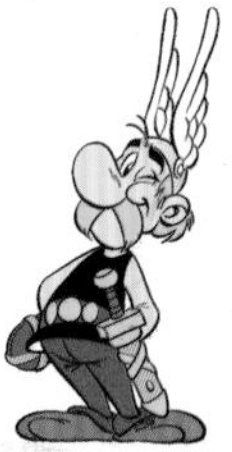

This is **Asterix**. A shrewd, little warrior of keen intellect... and superhuman strength. Asterix gets his superhuman strength from a magic potion. But he's not alone.

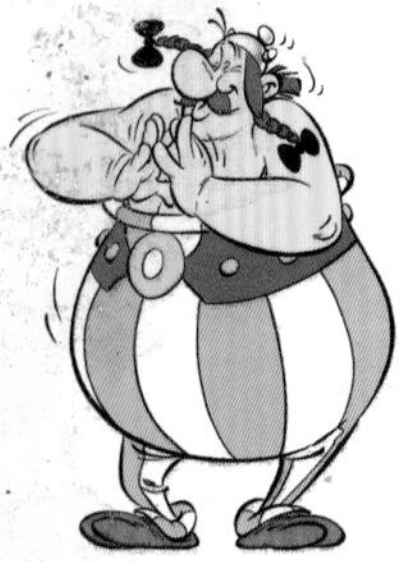

Obelix is Asterix's inseparable friend. He too has superhuman strength. He's a menhir (tall, upright stone monuments) deliveryman, he loves eating wild boar and getting into brawls. Obelix is always ready to drop everything to go off on a new adventure with Asterix.

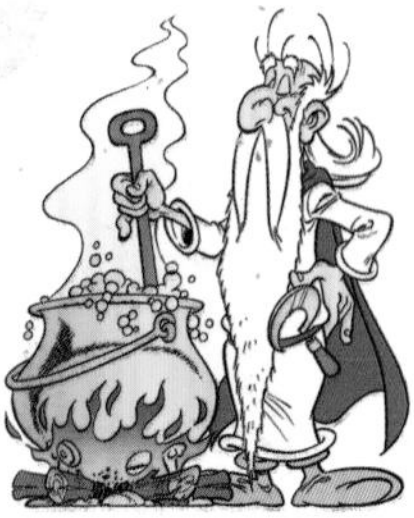

Panoramix, the village's venerable Druid, gathers mistletoe and prepares magic potions. His greatest success is the power potion. When a villager drinks this magical elixir he or she is temporarily granted super-strength. This is just one of the Druid's potions! And now you know why this small village can survive, despite seemingly impossible odds. While we're here, we may as well meet a few other Gauls...

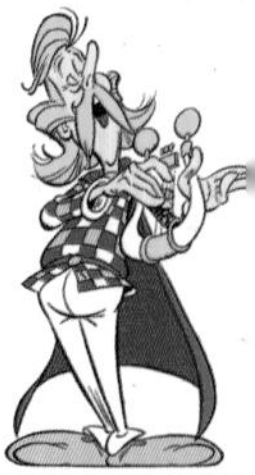

Cacofonix is the bard—the village poet. Opinions about his talents are divided: he thinks he's awesome, everybody else thinks he's awful, but when he doesn't say anything, he's a cheerful companion and well-liked...

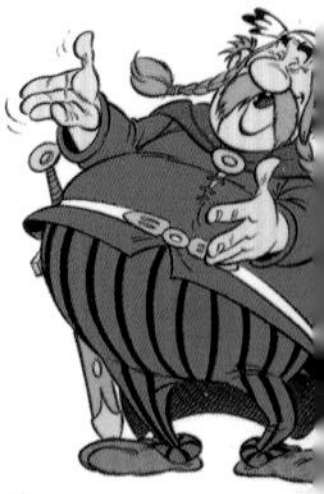

Vitalstatistix, finally, is the village's chief. Majestic, courageous, and irritable, the old warrior is respected by his men and feared by his enemies. Vitastatistix has only one fear: that the sky will fall on his head but, as he says himself, "That'll be the day!"

There are plenty more characters around here, but you'v met enough for now. In other words, that's Gaul, folks! I time we get back and wrap this up. Now, where did w put that time machine? Oh, there it is!

We're back, and we hope you enjoyed this trip back time to explore in 50 BC. For more information abo ASTERIX and his upcoming Papercutz graphic novels, ju go to papercutz.com.

As for THE LOUD HOUSE, we strongly suspect you wor want to miss the next graphic novel, "The Many Faces Lincoln Loud," which explores the many sides of our ma Linc!

Jim

STAY IN TOUCH!

EMAIL:	salicrup@papercutz.com
WEB:	papercutz.com
TWITTER:	@papercutzgn
INSTAGRAM:	@papercutzgn
FACEBOOK:	PAPERCUTZGRAPHICNOVELS
FANMAIL:	Papercutz, 160 Broadway, Suite 70 East Wing, New York, NY 10038

ORE GREAT GRAPHIC NOVEL SERIES AVAILABLE FROM PAPERCUTZ

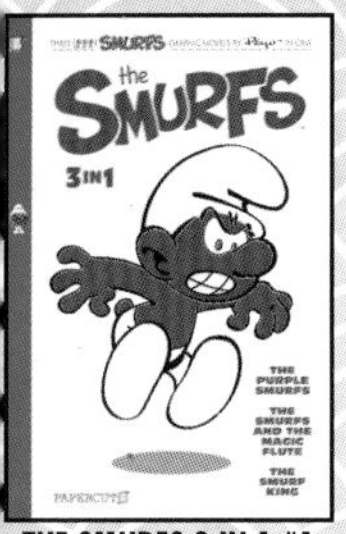
the SMURFS
3 IN 1
THE PURPLE SMURFS
THE SMURFS AND THE MAGIC FLUTE
THE SMURF KING
PAPERCUTZ
THE SMURFS 3 IN 1 #1

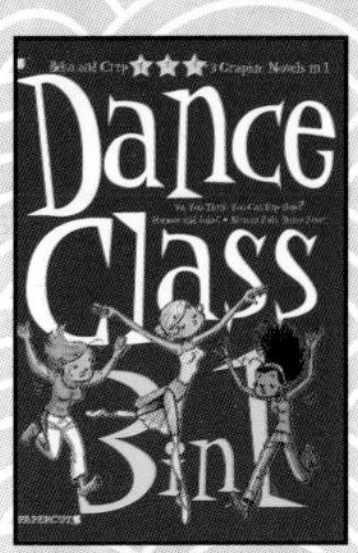
Dance Class
3 in 1
DANCE CLASS 3 IN 1 #1

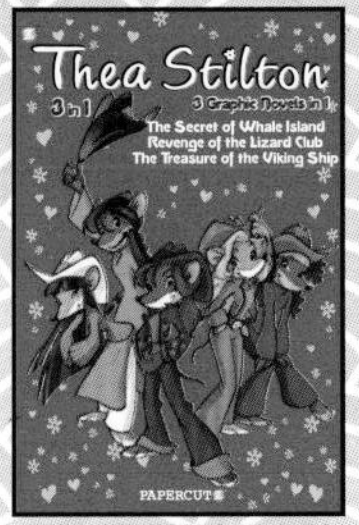
Thea Stilton
3 in 1
3 Graphic Novels in 1
The Secret of Whale Island
Revenge of the Lizard Club
The Treasure of the Viking Ship
PAPERCUTZ
THEA STILTON 3 IN 1 #1

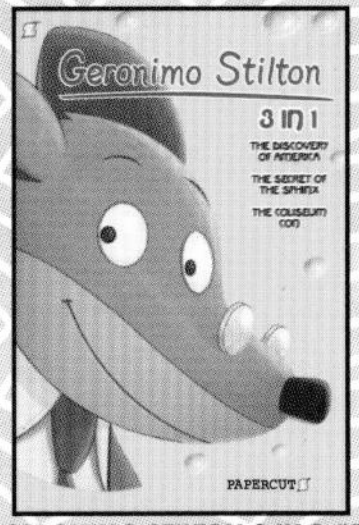
Geronimo Stilton
3 IN 1
PAPERCUTZ
GERONIMO STILTON 3 IN 1 #1

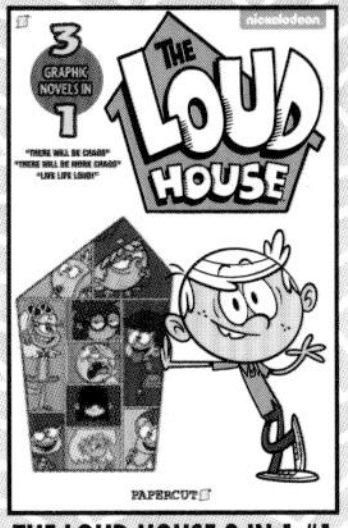
nickelodeon
3 GRAPHIC NOVELS IN 1
THE LOUD HOUSE
PAPERCUTZ
THE LOUD HOUSE 3 IN 1 #1

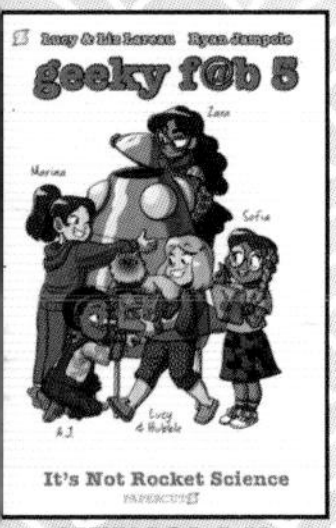
geeky f@b 5
It's Not Rocket Science
PAPERCUTZ
GEEKY F@B 5 #1

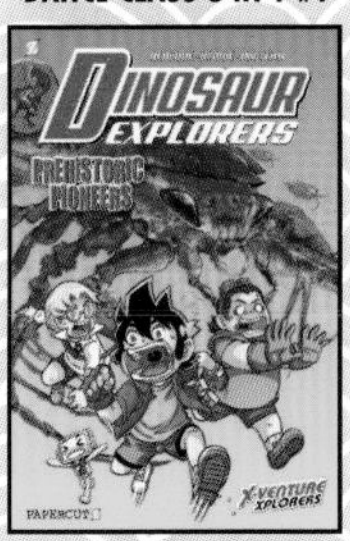
DINOSAUR EXPLORERS
PREHISTORIC PIONEERS
X-VENTURE EXPLORERS
PAPERCUTZ
DINOSAUR EXPLORERS #1

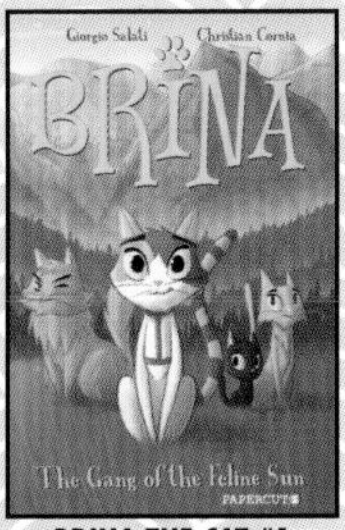
Giorgio Salati
Christian Cornia
BRINA
The Gang of the Feline Sun
PAPERCUTZ
BRINA THE CAT #1

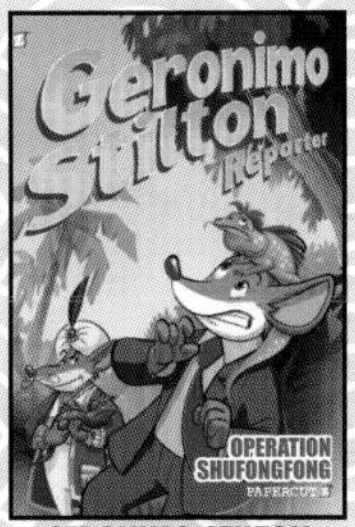
Geronimo Stilton
Reporter
OPERATION SHUFONGFONG
PAPERCUTZ
GERONIMO STILTON REPORTER #1

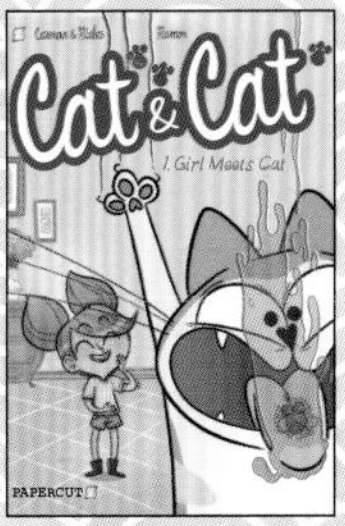
Cat & Cat
1. Girl Meets Cat
PAPERCUTZ
CAT & CAT #1

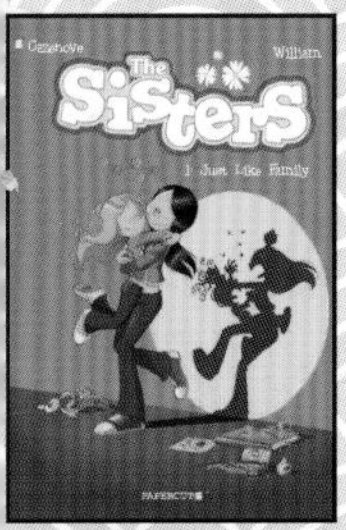
The Sisters
1. Just Like Family
PAPERCUTZ
THE SISTERS #1

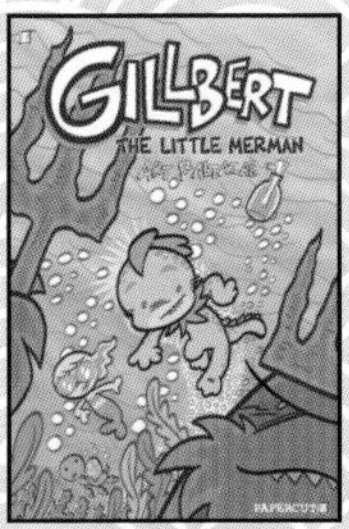
GILLBERT
THE LITTLE MERMAN
PAPERCUTZ
GILLBERT #1

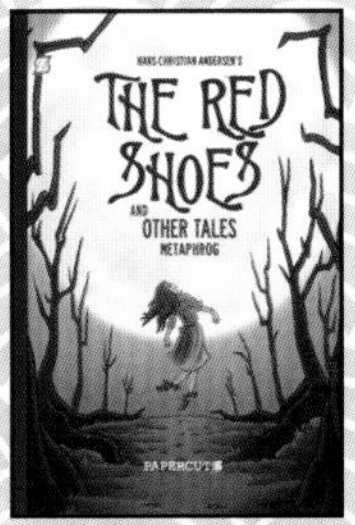
HANS CHRISTIAN ANDERSEN'S
THE RED SHOES
AND OTHER TALES
METAPHROG
PAPERCUTZ
THE RED SHOES

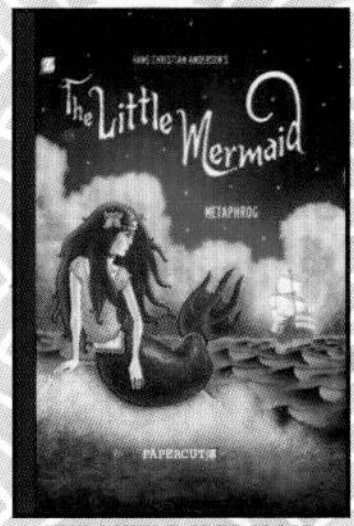
HANS CHRISTIAN ANDERSEN'S
The Little Mermaid
METAPHROG
PAPERCUTZ
THE LITTLE MERMAID

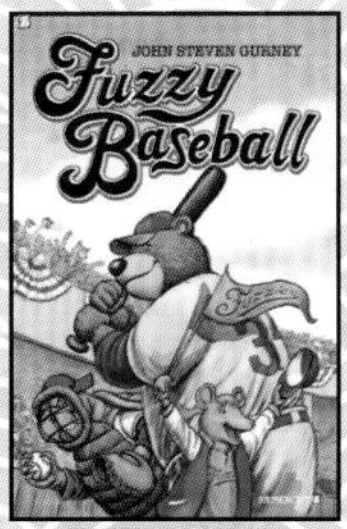
JOHN STEVEN GURNEY
Fuzzy Baseball
FUZZY BASEBALL

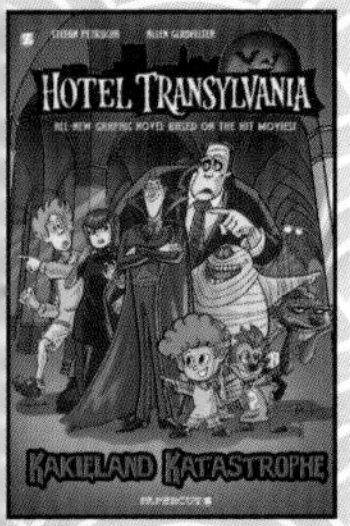
HOTEL TRANSYLVANIA
KAKIELAND KATASTROPHE
PAPERCUTZ
HOTEL TRANSYLVANIA #1

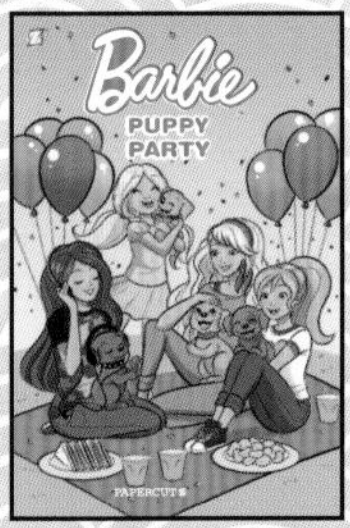
Barbie
PUPPY PARTY
PAPERCUTZ
BARBIE PUPPY PARTY #1

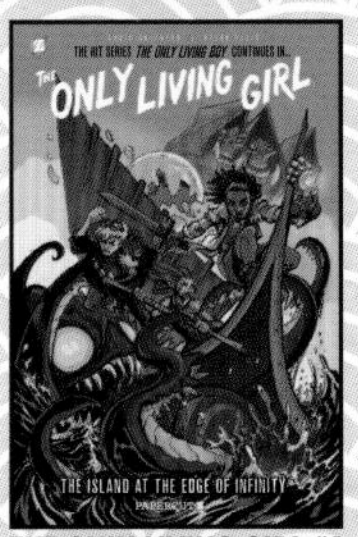
THE ONLY LIVING GIRL
THE ISLAND AT THE EDGE OF INFINITY
PAPERCUTZ
THE ONLY LIVING GIRL #1

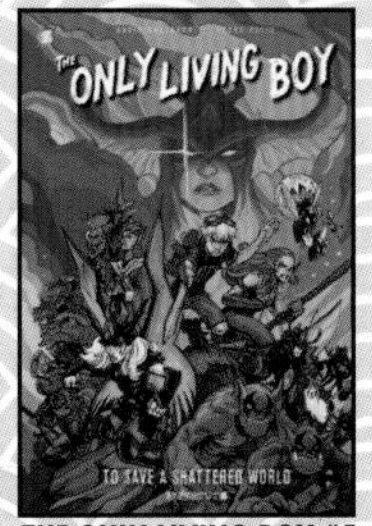
THE ONLY LIVING BOY
TO SAVE A SHATTERED WORLD
THE ONLY LIVING BOY #5

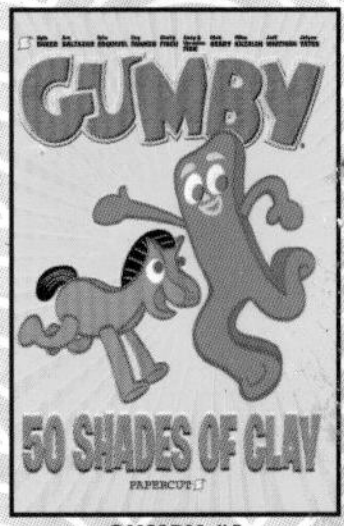
GUMBY
50 SHADES OF CLAY
PAPERCUTZ
GUMBY #1

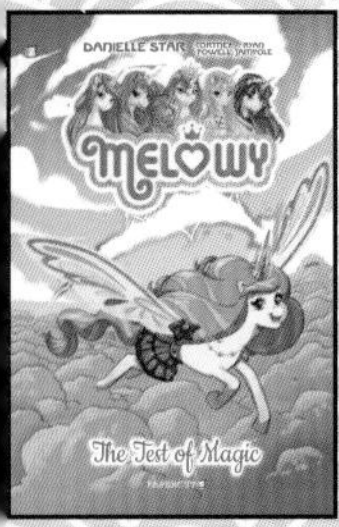
DANIELLE STAR
MELOWY
The Test of Magic
MELOWY #1

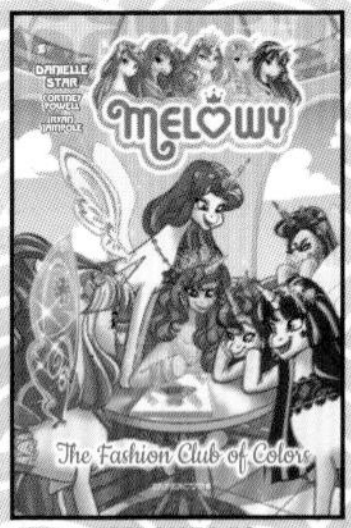
DANIELLE STAR
MELOWY
The Fashion Club of Colors
MELOWY #2

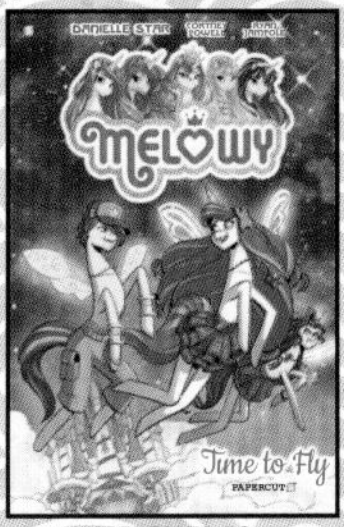
DANIELLE STAR
MELOWY
Time to Fly
PAPERCUTZ
MELOWY #3

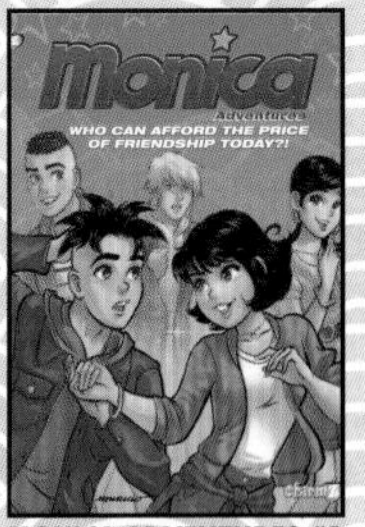
Monica
Adventures
WHO CAN AFFORD THE PRICE OF FRIENDSHIP TODAY?!
MONICA ADVENTURES #1

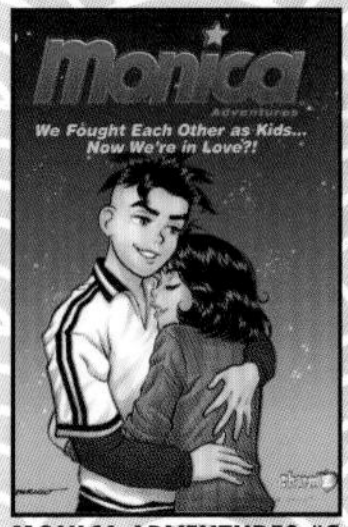
Monica
Adventures
We Fought Each Other as Kids... Now We're in Love?!
MONICA ADVENTURES #2

Go to papercutz.com for more!

'S, DANCE CLASS, BARBIE, GERONIMO STILTON, THE LOUD HOUSE, GEEKY FAB 5, DINOSAUR EXPLORERS, BRINA THE CAT, CAT & CAT, THE SISTERS, GILLBERT, THE RED SHOES, THE LITTLE MERMAID, FUZZY BASEBALL, HOTEL TRANSYLVANIA, THE ONLY LIVING BOY, THE ONLY LIVING GIRL, and GUMBY graphic novels are also available wherever e-books are sold.

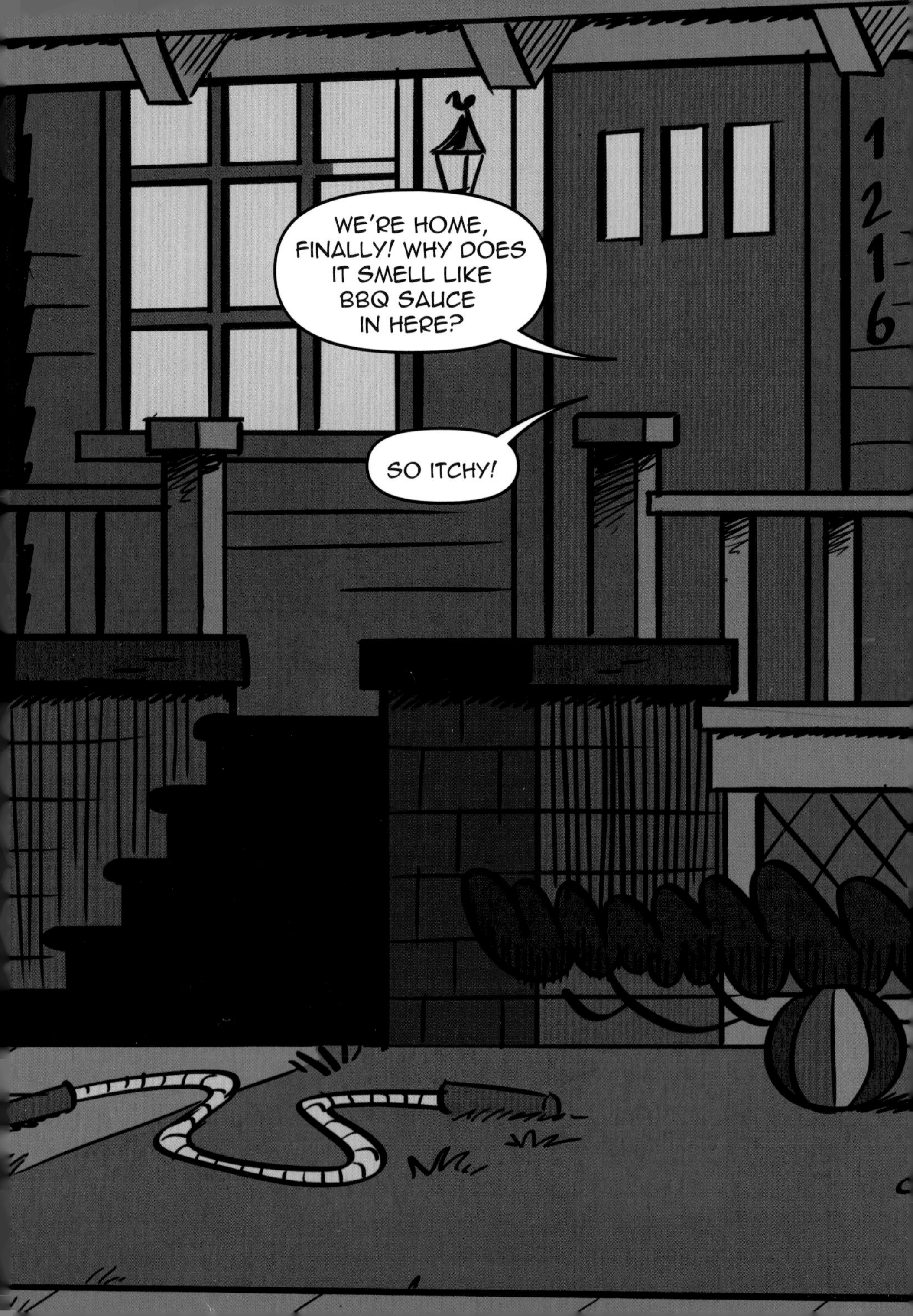
WE'RE HOME, FINALLY! WHY DOES IT SMELL LIKE BBQ SAUCE IN HERE?
SO ITCHY!
1216

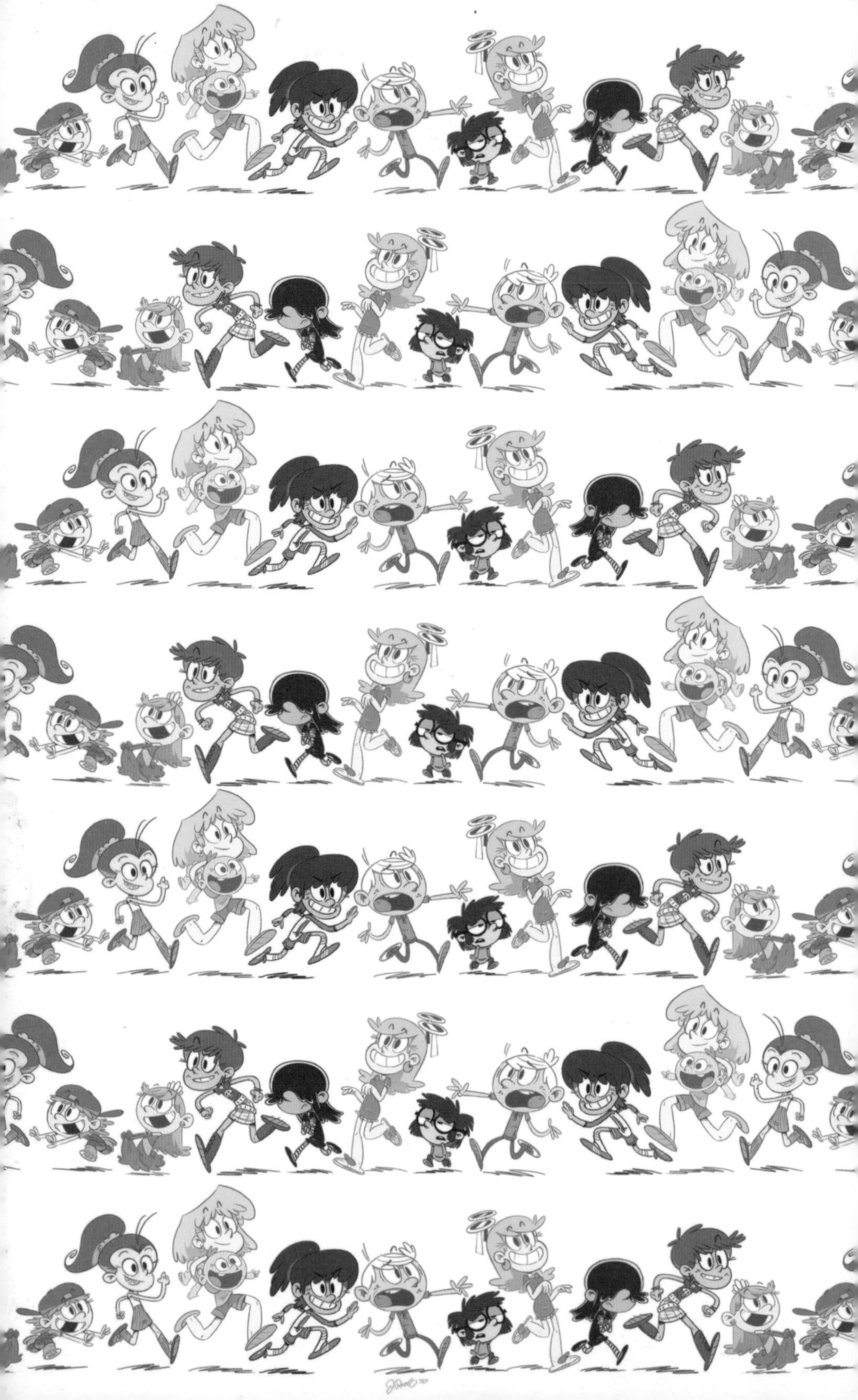